How Do You Spell
Abducted?

How Do You Spell
Abducted?

Cherylyn Stacey

Red Deer College Press

The Publishers
Red Deer College Press
56 Avenue & 32 Street Box 5005
Red Deer Alberta Canada T4N 5H5

Acknowledgments
Edited for the Press by Tim Wynne-Jones
Cover Art and Design by Jeff Hitch
Cover and text design by Dennis Johnson
Printed and bound in Canada by Webcom Limited for Red Deer College Press

5   4   3   2   1

Financial support provided by the Alberta Foundation for the Arts, a beneficiary of the Lottery Fund of the Government of Alberta, and by the Canada Council, the Department of Canadian Heritage and Red Deer College.

COMMITTED TO THE DEVELOPMENT OF CULTURE AND THE ARTS

Canadian Cataloguing in Publication Data
Stacey, Cherylyn, 1945–
How do you spell abducted?
(Northern lights young novels)
ISBN 0-88995-148-9
I. Title. II. Series.
PS8587.T232H69 1996   jC813'.54   C95-911208-1
PZ7.S72Ho 1996

For my daughters,
Cinnamon and Shea,
with all my love

How Do You Spell
Abducted?

CHAPTER 1

I STOPPED DEAD THE MINUTE I HEARD DAD SHOUTING. He shouted a lot, but this time was different . . . and worse. Mom and Dad had been divorced a whole year by now. He had no right to be in my living room shouting at my mother and making her cry.

"What do you mean 'It's better this way'? God, Ann, I miss you."

Uh-oh. He was trying that again. Dad regularly asked Mom to take him back.

"Tyler, you know we've done nothing but fight for the last ten years. Haven't you had enough?"

"Whatever happened to 'I promise to love, honor and obey till death do us part'?"

Dad was always good at telling other people what their duty was, but he got pretty mad when people tried to tell him he should settle down and get a steady job.

"I have the kids to think about," Mom said.

There was a long silence after that one. The hair on the back of my neck prickled as I listened to that long silence. Then Dad spoke in a low voice that was ten times scarier than shouting.

"Well, I've been thinking about the kids, too."

"Meaning?"

"I think about nothing but. I've got a right to see my

9

own kids. When you move to Kelowna, you take that right away from me. What kind of father would let someone do something like that?"

"Nobody's taking any rights away from you," Mom said in a high, cracked voice. "And besides, half the time you don't even bother to see the kids now."

"So you're moving to Kelowna to punish me."

"It's a good job with no shift work. That's best for the kids."

"What about me? I've got visiting rights!"

"What about you? I've got custody—"

"Because you got a smart lawyer who made me look bad."

"Because you never . . . Oh, never mind. No court's going to take the kids away from me because I'm moving to Kelowna. And we both know you wouldn't like having custody of the kids. Not one little bit."

"A fine time to pretend to worry about what I'd like!"

"Oh, for heaven's sake." Mom sounded more tired than scared now. "I wish you'd grow up."

Just then, my ten-year-old sister came around the corner of the house and started up the front steps. Paige has this annoying habit of thumping her way up and down stairs. Mom stopped talking the minute Paige hit the first step.

"Shh! Do you have to make such a racket?" I hissed under my breath.

"What? What did I do wrong?" Paige asked loudly.

That's Paige for you—she never knows what she's done wrong.

"I wanted to hear what they're talking about," I hissed.

"What who's talking about?"

You have to draw her a diagram to make her understand. I gave up and tried to walk into the house as though nothing was bothering me.

"Hi ya, there, Pet!" Dad said heartily. "Hot day to have to sit in school. Bet you're looking forward to the trip, eh?"

Pet. That meant he was talking to Paige. Since the divorce, he'd been calling me Deb, if he bothered to call me anything.

Paige ran to Dad and gave him a hug. Dad did his abominable snowman thing—"Mmm. Little gir-r-l-l. Me like little girl. Me take home to cave!"

Paige backed off, shrieking with laughter. Dad lumbered around like an awkward bear, grabbing for her and always just missing. Paige shrieked some more, even louder.

Finally, Dad caught her and did a bunch of stuff that looked like a bear mauling and eating somebody. Paige laughed and squirmed and screamed. But suddenly, Dad stopped what he was doing and looked up at me.

"So, Deb, where's your brother?"

"I don't know." I stood awkwardly just inside the door. I never understood how Paige could be so chummy with Dad. Maybe the things that happen to you before the age of eight don't make much of an impression. Maybe a year was all it had taken for Paige to forget those awful fights we used to lie awake listening to at night. Well, I hadn't forgotten, and I sure hadn't forgiven. If I hadn't been so scared of Dad, I'd have—

Well, come to think of it, I don't know what I'd have done. It made my knees shake just having to tell him I didn't know where Cory was.

Dad took a couple more chomps out of Paige and then turned back to me. "What do you mean, you don't know?"

"Why don't you ask Paige? They ride the bus together. One thing's for sure—he wasn't at school with me."

"Getting a bit mouthy, aren't you?" Dad asked quietly. "Where is Cory?" he asked Mom.

Mom looked at Paige.

"He's playing G.I. Joes with Jason," Paige said.

"That's kind of far for a five-year-old to have to walk home by himself," Dad said.

Give me a break! When I was five, I took the bus to kindergarten all by myself . . . even at forty below. To hear Dad talk, you'd think Cory wasn't safe walking half a mile down a quiet country road by himself in broad daylight in June.

Mom didn't say anything. After an awkward silence, Paige piped up. "Cory plays at Jason's lots, Daddy."

I looked at Mom. She was so pale that even her freckles didn't show.

"Looks to me as though these kids could do with some proper supervision," Dad said. "C'mon, Deb. Walk me to the car." He put a long arm heavily over my shoulder and walked me out the front door. "Getting tall," he said, giving my shoulder a squeeze. "You're going to be tall, like me."

He didn't need to remind me; I know I look a lot like him. I have his dark brown hair and eyes and his kind of babyishly handsome features. In fact, we've both been told we look like pictures of Elvis Presley. Paige, on the other hand, looks just like Mom. They both have reddish hair, freckles and big blue eyes.

And Cory? Well, Cory's got blond hair and brown eyes, and Dad says he's going to break a lot of hearts when he gets older. If anyone would know about breaking hearts, it would be Dad.

"So, is your mom seeing anyone yet?"

The question caught me off guard. "Huh?"

"It's been a year. I'll bet she's dating by now."

"Oh. No, she's not."

"Not at all? Maybe you and I have a different definition of dating. Do men come around at all?"

"Well, Mom's had to have the septic tank guys out here five times just this last month, if that's what you mean. . . ."

"No, that's not what I mean," he said, laughing heartily. "By men, I mean men friends."

Friends? He had to be kidding! Before the divorce, we moved so often that we never had a chance to make any. And in the year right after the divorce, Mom spent all her time either on duty at the hospital or taking care of us kids.

Anyway, something about the way he asked the question didn't sound right. It felt like he was pumping me for something he could blame Mom for.

In a minute, I was sure of it.

"So, who baby-sits you kids when she's at the hospital?"

Mom was forever warning me: If Dad ever asked that question, I was not to tell him I did most of the baby-sitting myself. Of course, it's legal to baby-sit when you're twelve, but I had been taking care of Paige and Cory even when I was eleven.

"It's been working out okay," I said, answering the first question and carefully avoiding the second. "Hey, isn't it great that Mom's going to work in a doctor's office?"

"What's so great about it? It means you're moving to Kelowna."

"Yeah. But no more shift work."

"Do you realize how far away from me you'll be living?"

"Um. I didn't think about that."

I was lying, the same way you jump back when you see a car bearing down on you fast. In my mind, I was always telling Dad to lay off us and leave us alone, but given a chance to actually say it out loud, here I was wimping out without even thinking. I hated the way I turned to jelly around him.

This wasn't to say that Dad wasn't handsome and charming and sometimes a lot of fun. But he had to get his own way all the time. And when he didn't get his way, he looked like he wanted to kill somebody. He could make you pretty tense when he lost his temper.

"Well, we still have this trip together before you go."

"Yeah."

"It'll be fun."

"Yeah."

My heart sank. In about a week, we had to go on holidays with Dad while Mom went to Kelowna and found us a place to live. I'd talked to Mom about getting out of it, but she said it couldn't be done. The court had given Dad visiting privileges, including two weeks with us in the summer.

It seems things like that couldn't be gotten out of. Even if we all said we didn't want to travel with Dad, we'd have to go to court and explain why to a judge. The worst of it was, there wasn't anything about Dad that would be easy to explain to a stranger. I mean, he didn't hit us or anything. Mom thought that people would think she'd been trying to turn us against him if we said we didn't want to be with him.

"Where are we going, Dad?"

"To the coast."

"You mean Grandma's?"

"Yeah. Why?"

"I dunno. Just wondering what we'd be doing, I guess."

"What a dorky question! We'll be having fun."

Would a judge understand if I told him Dad had a hairy every time I asked a simple question? Probably not. Probably that's what judges do with their own kids. Lots of people do. But not Mom, at least not when she's gotten some sleep and the plumbing's working.

I watched Dad climb into his beat-up brown Plymouth and struggle with the cranky old starter. For a long minute, it looked as though he wouldn't be able to get the car started, and we'd be stuck with him for an hour or more. But I willed the motor to turn over, and it finally roared to life with a great cloud of black smoke and three blasts like a shotgun going off.

"Well, Deb, be seeing you at the end of next week," Dad said.

"Sure, Dad."

"Well . . ." He looked like he didn't quite know what to do. "Be good." Suddenly, he reached out and pinched my cheek. "Still got more cheek than a chipmunk, I see. I swear, when they start selling stocks in cheeks, you'll have your fortune made."

I used to like that joke when I was a kid. It feels like that was a hundred years ago.

Next thing I knew, I stood in a cloud of dust, and Dad was roaring up our weedy, rutted driveway with a funny clanking sound that I could hear long after he was out of sight behind the trees. I didn't realize I was holding my breath until I let it out. Just then, I looked back up at the ramshackle two-story farmhouse we'd lived in since the divorce, and I saw a flash of white at the living room window. It disappeared and Mom appeared at the door, looking as relieved as I felt.

"He can't get us can he?"

"What do you mean?" Mom asked sharply, looking everywhere but at me.

"I mean, he can't get custody, can he?"

Now Mom was looking right at me, and she was doing it in a queer, intent way that was positively scary. "There is nothing to worry about, Debbie," she said slowly and carefully. "Please believe me. I won't let anything bad happen. You have nothing to worry about."

Well, that settled it. Something was wrong and Mom was scared stiff. She says stuff like that only when it's big and important and scary; the rest of the time we talk like friends.

Mom reached over and put her hand over mine. Without realizing what I was doing, I had begun to scratch a rash on the inside of my left elbow. It always flares up when I'm nervous.

"Don't," Mom said. "It'll only make it worse."

"I wish you would tell me what's going on."

"There's nothing to tell," Mom said, avoiding my eyes.

But that night, after we were all in bed, she phoned somebody from work and told her.

"Guess who was over here throwing a temper tantrum today," Mom said. "Can you believe it? All of a sudden, he's just got to be somebody's father, and I'm a horrible person to be keeping him from his kids. If I had any sense, I'd let him take them and see just how much trouble three kids can be! Wouldn't it just teach him a lesson if I did?"

I sat at the top of the dark, steep stairway, hugging my knees and listening.

"Oh, I know it's all aimed at me. . . . Don't think I don't see through him. And don't think I'm happy about sending the kids off with him for two weeks. . . . What can I do? . . . I've already talked to my lawyer about it, and she says a guy has to do something seriously wrong before he can lose his visiting privileges."

I listened till Mom was done, but I didn't learn anything else. Finally, I could tell she was getting ready to hang up, so I snuck quietly back to the room I shared with Paige.

"Will you please quit scratching like that! You're driving me crazy," Paige said after a minute or two.

"Shut up and go to sleep."

"I *was* asleep. Put some Mazon on and go to sleep yourself." She got up on one elbow and squinted blearily at the clock. "You creep! It's eleven o'clock." She leaned over and gave me a hard whack on the arm. Even half asleep, Paige can deliver one that hurts.

"Ow. Quit hitting me, Paige. It's not my fault that I itch." I guessed that Mom was coming up the stairs, so I said it loudly enough for a person on the stairs to hear.

"Well, it's not my fault either. Go to sleep."

"What's going on?" Suddenly, Mom was at the door. "Why are you hitting Debbie, Paige? Why aren't you asleep?"

"I wasn't hitting her," Paige said.

"Liar!" I yelled.

"I mean," Paige explained, "that I only hit her once. She woke me up, Mom. I was asleep and she woke me up. Now I'll probably never get back to sleep."

"For heaven's sake, Debbie, stop scratching! Go put some Mazon on that eczema and then settle down."

"How can I settle down when she's hitting me all the time?"

"I'm not hitting her all the time!" Paige said. "I just want to sleep. She's driving me crazy. She scratches so hard she shakes the bed."

Paige *was* hitting me all the time—and had been ever since she turned two—but I could see that she and Mom agreed about the scratching thing, so now wasn't the time to argue about it. Still, it wouldn't do to give up too easily. Mom might get the impression that Paige was right and I was wrong.

"Nobody cares that Paige is always beating on me," I mumbled.

"Oh, for heaven's sake. Cut it out!" Mom yelled. "You're driving me crazy! I'll never in a million years understand why you two can't get along. I should just lock you both in a room and let you go at it till you drop."

Paige began to cry quietly. Paige hugs easily and cries easily. I don't know how bad she really felt, being yelled at like that. All I know is that I felt awful, and part of what made me feel awful was that I'd gotten Paige into trouble. Of course, it was what I'd hoped for. I only wish she got yelled at every time she hit me. But it did seem too bad that she'd been sound asleep and now she was being bawled out—all in the space of two minutes.

I don't cry. Not ever. I stomped off to the bathroom to get the Mazon and then stomped back to bed again, letting Mom know just how mad I was and that I wasn't going to forgive or forget.

When I got back, Mom was hugging Paige and crying. That did it. It made me feel as though the whole world was against me. I got into bed and turned my face to the wall.

"Good night, Debbie," Mom said after a minute or two. "Sorry I blew my stack."

I didn't answer. It takes me a few minutes to get over being mad. But this particular night, I didn't have a few minutes. Mom stood over me twenty seconds, twenty-five max.

"Sometimes you are the most irritating person I know," she said, and turned and went out of the room.

Nice going, Deb. You irritate Mom more than anyone. More than Paige. More than Dad. Five minutes of thinking about that and the itch was spreading all over.

CHAPTER 2

A WHOLE WEEK BEFORE WE LEFT, CORY PACKED HIS ADIDAS bag with pajamas, comic books—which he couldn't read but knew off by heart—and his hamster, Gretel. These were the things he thought you should never leave home without. He never went anywhere without Gretel in his pocket.

When Mom told him that he couldn't take Gretel, he began by trying to explain to her that Gretel had to come. Then he ended up hiding Gretel and her luggage in dumb places that Mom twigged to right away. Each time she found him out and insisted that Gretel had to go over to Jason's now, Cory set out with dragging steps in the general direction of Jason's house . . . and the hamster showed up in a new hiding place the next day.

"You don't understand," Mom said, getting down on her knees and gathering Cory into her arms. "Hamsters hate to travel. They get drafts easily. And if she ever got away, she'd be almost impossible to catch."

"But we're buds," Cory said. "And, besides, Jason's going away."

"Just to their cottage at the lake. That's different."

"Gretel wants to see stuff."

"What kind of stuff?"

"Well . . . the ocean. I told her I'd show her the ocean."

20

"Believe me, Cory, when she sees Jason's lake, she's going to think she's seeing the ocean."

Cory brightened, but then he leaned over and whispered something in Mom's ear.

"What? I can't hear you."

"I said," Cory said loudly, "that I'll miss her."

"Of course you will. Just like I'll miss you. Does that mean you don't want to go on holidays with Dad?"

Cory shook his head.

"Well, then, I guess we'll all just have to say our good-byes and be patient till we see each other again."

Suddenly, Cory was hugging Mom tight enough to choke her. But it was just a slight case of homesickness, and it passed quickly because he was going to be with his dad just like Jason was always with his dad. Besides, Dad was taking him on holidays, and he'd never been on holidays before.

I DON'T THINK any of us had the slightest idea of what that would be like.

Dad put Cory in the front seat with him, and Paige and me in the back. Paige got restless right away and squirmed all over the place, putting her feet on me, digging her sharp little elbows into me, bouncing on the seat. . . . Finally, I couldn't stand it anymore and gave her a shove. Of course she gave me an even harder shove and then started pinching and tickling me.

"Cut it out, Paige!"

"I didn't do anything."

"Yes, you did. You know you did. You stuck your finger in my ear."

"Did not. You were trying to hit me with your head."

"Hey, settle down, you two," Dad warned.

"This is my side of the car," I said, marking everything to the left of center. "Stay on your own side. And that means keep your hands on your own side, too."

Right away, Paige sat as close to the center line as she possibly could. Pretty soon, she was creeping over so she was a little on my side.

"You're on my side, Paige," I said. I wanted Dad to know what she was doing, so I said it loud enough for him to hear.

"I said to cut out the fighting," Dad said. "Now I don't want to hear another word from either of you. Understand?"

"But—"

"Not another word!"

That wasn't fair. I hadn't done anything, but I was getting blamed. And, worse yet, now that Paige saw how it was with Dad, she knew she could do anything to make me mad without getting into trouble, as long as she did it quietly. She began to make faces at me.

I tried to ignore her, but she inched closer and closer, knowing I didn't want to complain out loud. I turned my back to her and looked out the window. She tapped me on the back over and over again.

That did it. I wasn't going to take this another minute. And, come to think of it, if I didn't want to attract Dad's attention by making a noise, neither would Paige. Right?

Wrong!

I aimed an elbow at her shoulder but caught her on the chin. She let out a howl of pain, and Dad reached back with a folded-up map and started swatting at both of us.

"It's not fair. She hit me," Paige said, scrambling back

over to her side of the car and leaving me to take most of Dad's unaimed blows.

"Aw, c'mon, you guys," Dad pleaded. "Give me a break, will you? We're supposed to be having fun. I've got a tough job here, driving, and I need for you to help me out. How would you guys like to have to drive hours and hours with a couple of kids fighting in the back seat?"

Paige stuck her tongue out at me and shook her head from side to side. I gave her the finger. She made a chopping motion at the elbow that said "Up yours . . . up to here." I went one better with a chopping motion at my waist. She topped me with a chop to her forehead. Since I didn't know how to top that, I turned back to looking out the window. Paige sat back and soon fell fast asleep.

I sat there wondering what Mom was doing. Putting the last of her clothes in a suitcase? Checking the doors and windows before leaving? Loading the car? Thinking about us?

Suddenly, the car coughed and died. Dad steered it over to the side of the road and let it coast to a stop.

"Damn!"

"What's the matter, Dad?" Cory asked. "Why're we stopping? Won't the car go?"

Dad looked tired and discouraged. "Damn, damn, damn, damn."

He pounded on the steering wheel, then got out and kicked the side of the car. We sat there staring at him, so he managed to dredge up a weak grin. "Hang tough. I'll have it fixed in a minute."

Paige woke up with a jerk. "Hey, how come we're stopped?"

"Oh, look," Cory said, pointing.

Fifteen black-and-white cows were running across a

field to get a better look at us. Their huge udders swung as they ran, like purses on ladies running to catch a bus. They charged right up to the fence, then stood chewing wads of grass and looking at us with big, soft, brown eyes.

"Easy to tell we're the most exciting thing that's happened to them all week," Paige said.

Dad had the hood up and was muttering louder and louder.

"Maybe he'll take us back home to Mom," I said hopefully.

"No," Cory hollered. "I don't want to go home. I want to go on a trip!"

"Don't worry," Paige reassured him, "we will. We'll see Grandma and the ocean and a double-decker Ferris wheel."

Cory opened the front door and jumped out to get a better look at the cows. I was thinking that was a good idea, after sitting so long, when suddenly Dad plunked Cory back down in his seat and said to me through clenched teeth, "What do you think you're doing?"

I had thought I was just sitting there quietly, but the way Dad said it, I thought for a minute that he could read my mind. Was I in trouble just for thinking of getting out of the car?

"Do you have rocks in your head? How could you let a little kid get out of the car on a two-lane highway. He could have been killed."

"He was just going over to look at the cows," Paige said.

"Don't you talk back to me, young lady."

"I wasn't talking back to you."

Dad brought the flat of his hand down hard on the headrest, making us all jump a little. But then he pulled himself together, rubbed his head hard and tried again in a different tone of voice.

"Think how I'd feel if something happened to you. Think how you'd feel if your little brother got hurt because you didn't take care of him. Now just sit here until I get this thing fixed. Don't move a muscle or say a word. And," he pointed his finger at us in the back seat, "I'm holding you two responsible for Cory. Understand?"

We sat there silently, eyes straight ahead, until he was back under the hood of the car.

"What I don't understand," Paige finally whispered, "is how we're supposed to stop Cory from getting out of the car if we're not supposed to do or say anything."

"Mental telepathy, I guess."

Paige giggled.

"But I want to get out," Cory said.

"Well, you can't, so just shut up about it," I snapped.

"Hey, Cor," Paige said, "how about a game of I Spy?"

Yeah, sure. Make me look bad. I started to scratch.

How long was fourteen days anyway? I worked on that for a while and came up with something a bit over three hundred hours. So we had something like two hundred ninety-seven to go. More or less.

An old man in a beat-up brown truck pulled in ahead of us and called back to Dad, "Having trouble?"

Dad laughed. "Usually she just needs a kick in the pants to show her who's boss, but today . . ."

"It'll be this goldarned heat."

"Yeah, it's hard on the carburetor."

Dad stepped into view from behind the raised hood. He looked young and scared. "But I figure if anyone can make the adjustments, it's got to be me. I'm the one who knows this old girl and her crotchets."

The old man came over and peered nearsightedly under the hood. "I dunno. Maybe you're right. Want me to call a tow truck?"

"Heck, no! No, we'll be okay. I know what I'm doing."

"You sure? I don't mind."

"Naw, no problem. Really."

Dad didn't look as sure as he sounded, but the old man bought it. He turned and peered into the car. "What good little kids," he said. "A car ride is bad enough, but sitting in a car that isn't moving is murder."

Dad laughed. "Oh, they don't mind a bit."

"Really good kids!" The old man turned and shambled back to his truck. "Well, good luck."

With a spray of gravel, he pulled away, leaving us feeling more alone than ever. Even the cows got bored with us and wandered away.

When we couldn't stand I Spy anymore, we tried a game where we watched the cars passing us. You got points for spotting things like convertibles, big trucks, campers with bicycle racks and green or yellow cars. But it got hot in the car, and we got too sleepy to keep our mind on the traffic. I was so hungry my stomach hurt. Paige said her mouth was so dry she could hardly talk.

"I wonder what time it is," Paige said. "I bet it's four o'clock."

"Who knows? All I know is I'm hungry," Cory said. "I could eat a horse."

"I wonder how much longer this is going to take," I said.

"I'll ask Dad," Cory said.

"Cory."

"What?"

"Don't ask him that. He'll get mad."

We argued about that for a while—whether Cory should ask Dad what time it was or whether someone else should ask him and if it sounded snarky to ask him how much longer he expected to be.

"I'm not scared," Cory said. "And I want to know."

"No. Don't do it," I said. Dad had started out swearing under his breath, but he'd been getting louder and louder as time went by. By this time, a steady stream of unprintable words were pouring from beneath the hood of the car.

"Oh, you're such a sissy, Debbie," Paige said.

"Hey, Dad," Cory called out.

"Yeah, what is it?"

"How much longer do we have to be here?"

Dad straightened up and came over to the window with a wrench in his hand. "Here," he said, holding out the wrench. "You fix it. You think you could do it faster than me? Well, go ahead—fix it! . . . Well?" Dad shook the wrench at Cory. "No? Then shut up and let me get the thing done."

He walked back to the front of the car, and we slumped as comfortably as we could and just waited.

It must have been another hour before we got going, then nearly another hour before we reached the little town of Rocky Mountain House. By the time Dad pulled up in front of the Dairy Queen, it was five o'clock and we hadn't eaten since breakfast.

He pulled into the drive-through, ordered us all hamburgers, french fries and cokes, and drove out as soon as he got them. He polished off his burger in two minutes flat as he drove a few blocks to a hotel with a beer parlor.

"I'll just be a minute," he said, getting out of the car. "Keep the doors locked, don't talk to strangers and—

whatever you do—do not get out of the car. Understand?"

We all said we understood, and Dad disappeared into the beer parlor. I couldn't blame him for that, after all those hours he'd just spent fixing the car on a hot day in the middle of nowhere, but what about us! We needed to get out and stretch. And worst of all, we needed a bathroom. For Cory, being so small, it was especially hard.

"I'm going to bust my gut," he said after about ten minutes.

"I'm going to bust my gut, and I'm going to do it now," he said after half an hour.

"How much longer can Dad be?" Paige replied. "For sure he'll be back in two minutes. Two at the most."

We did some countdowns from ten to zero, pointing dramatically at the beer parlor door with a big "ta-da" that was supposed to be followed immediately by the door opening and Dad coming out. Five ta-das later, there was still no sign of Dad.

Paige nudged me and pointed to tears on Cory's cheeks. The kid was really hurting.

"That does it," I said. "Cory, I'm taking you into the hotel. There'll be a washroom there."

"No," Cory said. "You said Dad would be out in a minute. He'll be mad as heck if he comes back and we're gone."

"He'll understand," I said.

But we weren't really sure about that.

"How about if Debbie takes you behind the hotel?" Paige suggested. "It won't take long, and you won't have gone far."

"He said not to get out of the car, period."

"Well, we've got to do something," I said, biting my lip. We watched the door of the beer parlor some more.

"I think I'm going to wet my pants," Cory whispered.

I got so mad at Dad that my ears buzzed, but I still didn't know what to do. It's a good thing Paige, at least, was thinking straight.

"Here," she said, thrusting an empty coke container at Cory. "Go in that."

Cory never even argued. He just did it. We put the lid on and put the thing in the bag down on the floor with the other containers from supper. A few minutes later, Dad pitched it without even knowing what was in it.

With the car fixed, supper in us, a chance to use a washroom at a service station and—best of all—Dad feeling good with a few beers in him, I was sure that the worst was over.

But I was wrong. The day ended with Dad pulling into a little campground out in the middle of nowhere and telling us that we were going to sleep in the car that night. The mosquitoes were fierce. We only had two blankets—a picnic blanket and a dirty, old, car-seat blanket—and it got colder and colder till we couldn't stop shivering. And the most uncomfortable bed in the whole entire world has to be the back seat of a car.

Because it stayed light till eleven, I started a letter to Mom after I went to bed in the back seat. I knew I'd probably never send it because she wasn't going to be home anyway, but it made me feel better to get some things off my chest to her.

Oh, Mom, it's the pits being with Dad!!! I don't care what the courts say—nobody should've made me go with him. Let the little kids go with him. They wanted to. But I should be with you. It's just like I knew it would be. He bosses me around and never listens to a thing I say.

I imagined Mom stroking my hair. "And if you weren't there, who would take care of Cory and Paige? He hasn't got the least idea what little kids need."

A few minutes later, I actually fell asleep.

Just as the first gray light of dawn made it possible to see that Paige was awake now, too, she leaned over and whispered in my ear, "Are we having fun yet?"

She was learning fast.

CHAPTER 3

THINGS DIDN'T GET BETTER; THEY GOT WEIRDER. DAD'S idea of a good holiday appeared to be driving hour after hour in dead silence. We didn't stop in Banff or Lake Louise. We didn't stop at the enchanted castle Cory begged to see. Hot and tired as we were, we went right by Shuswap Lake without even wetting our feet.

"When are we getting there?" Cory finally asked.

"Getting where?" Dad asked, starting to bristle.

"I don't know. Where we're going."

"Kids these days!" Dad said with disgust. "What's the matter with you? Can't you drive a few hundred miles without complaining? When I was a kid, we drove all the way to California in three days. That meant twelve hours a day of driving . . . and no complaining either. My dad wouldn't have stood for it."

"I thought we were going to see Grandma," Cory said.

"We are," Dad said.

By this time, I could've cared less where we were going. I ached all over, and I just wanted this horrible car ride to end.

Long after supper was overdue and my stomach had given up reminding me of that fact, we pulled into Grandma Adaskin's driveway in Surrey, British Columbia. Grandma came running out of the house.

"Tyler, thank God you're here! You're so late! I finally gave up on you and put the supper things away." She looked us over with a shrewd eye. "You kids look famished."

"What nonsense," Dad said laughing. "They're perfectly all right."

I was scared that Grandma would believe Dad and drop the idea of feeding us, but Cory took care of that. He threw himself into Grandma's arms like a tiny football tackle and said in no uncertain terms, "I am hungry. I'm hungrier than I've ever been before in my whole life. So are Paige and Debbie."

Grandma laughed. "Well, we'll have to do something about that, won't we? How about some homemade soup and some of my super-dooper cinnamon buns?"

We gobbled down supper as fast as we could stuff the food in our mouths. Grandma turned worried brown eyes on Dad with a hint of accusation in them.

"Tyler, you could have fed them."

Dad gave us a dirty look and then flashed a warm, funny smile at Grandma.

"Hey, give me a break! I'm a bit out of practice at this fathering bit. And, anyway, they couldn't have been that hungry—they never said a word about it to me." He managed to sound pitiful and lovable and funny all at the same time, and Grandma just ate it up.

"My poor baby," Grandma crooned. "Has it been terrible for you?"

"It's been hell," he said. "I'll tell you about it later."

After supper, Dad took us out to see where he used to play Robin Hood when he was a kid. There was still an old tree house perched lopsided high in a big elm tree. Dad helped us get up there, then climbed up after us.

Crouched with his knees up around his ears, he told us stories about getting in trouble with his dad over school and about the time he ran away from home and moved into the tree house. The way he told the story, we laughed till our sides hurt. And we didn't let him stop telling stories till long after dark.

Back at the house, Paige and Cory fell asleep right away, but I was so tired I couldn't seem to stop tossing and turning. That's how it happened that I was the only one to hear snatches of the conversation between Dad and Grandma.

"Money? How much? Why?"

That was Grandma's voice, high and anxious. I couldn't hear Dad's answer. He kept his voice low—a steady droning that sounded more like the hum of a bee than a person talking.

"Oh, Tyler, I don't think that's a good idea!"

What could be making her sound so upset?

"But think of the children!"

"Think of me." That was the only time Dad forgot himself enough to raise his voice loud enough to be heard.

More droning. Much more droning. Somewhat later, Grandma said she was worried—worried sick. I could hear a sudden rattle of cups and spoons on saucers, and I was pretty sure Dad must have brought his hand down hard on the kitchen table. After that, Grandma said no a few times but with more doubt and less strength.

Finally, she said, "I don't agree, but you are my son. Of course, I'll help you all I can."

They talked a long time after that, and sometime before they finished, I drifted off to sleep.

The next day, we slept in so late that Grandma had

already been out and back before we got downstairs. To the bank, I guessed. We walked into the kitchen just as she was handing a big envelope over to Dad. It looked like money.

She looked pretty unhappy. Dad looked extremely pleased and more cheerful than I had seen him for a long time.

"Well, you rascals," he said, turning to us. "Finally up, are you? Come here and give me a hug."

I gave him the economy model, which was all I figured he had coming to him, but the little kids were in the mood for some serious snuggling. Dad gave it to them, and, watching him, Grandma quickly lost the worried look she had come in with. Dad glanced up at one point, and they smiled happily at each other.

"Oh, Tyler," she exclaimed. "I haven't been fair to you at all. I'm so sorry."

"What on earth are you talking about?" Dad asked. "You've always been the best mom in the world. If I can be half as good a dad, I'll be happy."

"You'll be a great father," Grandma said, and she just stood there beaming peacefully at him—until, that is, Dad said we'd be leaving the next day.

"So soon? Can't you stay at least a week?"

"You know I can't do that."

"Well, then, a couple of days. Lord knows when I'll see you again or even hear from you. . . ."

"You know why I have to be on my way."

I looked from one to the other, trying to make sense of Grandma's tragic tone of voice and Dad's low warning. Soon I had even more to wonder about.

At the American border the next day, we were in a left-hand lineup to go through the border checkpoint when Paige spotted Mr. and Mrs. Eden in a right-hand lineup a couple of cars back of us. The Edens had been our neighbors just before the divorce.

"Hey, there's Mr. Eden!" Paige yelled. "Honk your horn, Dad. I don't think he's seen us."

Dad craned his neck to get a look at the car Paige was pointing to. It sure looked like Mr. Eden's blue station wagon.

"I don't think that's them," Dad said.

"Sure it is," Cory said. "I'll prove it." He opened the door and was just starting to jump out when Dad grabbed him by the seat of the pants and hauled him back inside.

"Don't ever do that again. Now just sit still. That isn't Mr. Eden, so forget it."

"But it is," Paige said, close to tears. "I know it is. Why don't you believe me?"

"Sit down," Dad said. "Boy, what an imagination!"

Dad didn't look back over his shoulder again, but he did keep looking in the rearview mirror, and he kept drumming his long, thin fingers on the steering wheel. Also, he began crowding the van ahead of us, as though he could make the line move faster by pushing.

I glanced back once or twice. The right-hand line was moving faster than ours and the blue station wagon was getting closer. It was Mr. Eden, all right. Paige and Cory never took their eyes off the station wagon for a minute, and Cory started to roll down his window as it got quite close.

"And just what do you think you're doing?"

"I'm going to say hi," Cory said.

"No you're not."

"But—"

"Subject closed."

Just then it was our turn to talk to the customs agent.
"How long you folks planning to be in the States?"

Dad gave him a big smile. "About a week."

"The wife not along?"

"'Fraid not. She's starting a new job. Finally getting off shift work. Too good an opportunity to let pass."

The American bent down and looked long and hard at each one of us. "How you kids doing?"

"Great! We're going to the ocean!" Cory said.

"That so? Bet you like to swim."

"Oh, we never get a chance to," Paige said. "This is our first holiday."

"Well, maybe you'll learn," the man said. "Got birth certificates?" he asked Dad.

Dad handed them over and started to ask how the weather had been, but the customs man was busy checking our certificates out against some kind of list, so Dad let it drop and just watched.

When Dad finally got the birth certificates back, he laughed. "They're too young to be robbing banks."

"That's for sure. But they're not too young to be in our data bank if they've been reported missing."

"Oh. Yeah, it's sad the way—"

But the man had lost all interest in us and was waving us on, so Dad put his foot down hard on the gas and left the customs checkpoint to gasp for air in a cloud of blue smoke.

I looked back at the Edens' station wagon. A week in the States; ten days till we'd be home. About two hundred and forty hours. Well, time wasn't exactly racing, but at least it was passing.

We stopped at a Motel Six in Yakima that evening, and Dad took us down to the swimming pool before supper. There he proved to Paige and Cory's total amazement that it's possible to float on your back if you just keep your head and don't panic.

Later, while he was making macaroni and cheese for our supper and Paige and Cory had the living room couch already made into a bed and were sprawled all over it, watching television, I started to pour myself a glass of milk and then stopped, held by the pictures of kids on the outside of the milk carton. They were ordinary-looking kids, and under each picture was a short bit about how old they were and when they had last been seen.

Missing kids. I read the entire carton from top to bottom and from corner to corner, and when I was done, I knew without having to think about it that we had just gone missing ourselves. Only nobody knew that yet, except Dad. And Grandma.

I looked at Dad frying hot dogs to go with the macaroni. He looked just like usual.

"Hey, Deb . . ."

I jumped, feeling guilty.

"Peel us four carrots, will you?"

I began to peel carrots with hands that shook.

It fit together. Dad's bad mood and Grandma's worrying and how Dad had avoided Mr. Eden and kept driving all the time without doing any holiday sorts of things. But being kidnapped . . . surely that was something that happened to other kids, not to me and my brother and sister. Something that awful couldn't happen to us.

Or could it? The next day, I figured out our direction by checking the names of towns we had passed on a map that had slipped under the front seat. We were driving east again. Driving east didn't make a whole lot of sense if Dad was taking us to the coast. If he'd changed his mind, why wasn't he saying?

Okay. Calm down, Debbie, I told myself. Just calm down and think.

Somewhere just outside of Spokane, Dad stopped for a beer and left us kids to wait for him in the car again. With a pounding heart, I listened to the same instructions he'd given at Rocky Mountain House—don't get out; don't talk to anybody—and then I jumped out of the car almost as soon as the bar door closed behind him.

Paige and Cory threw hairies.

"Debbie, are you crazy?"

"I won't be more than two minutes," I said.

Cory stared at me. Paige tried to grab me.

"He'll kill you."

"If he finds out. But he won't. You know he's going to be in there for an hour. . . . I promise you I won't be more than two minutes."

"Why? What're you going to do?"

"Never mind. I'll explain when I get back."

Well, it took longer than two minutes, that's for sure. First I had to find a pay phone. Then I had to change some of my twenty dollars spending money into coins. But finally I was ready to call Mom.

I pressed the zero for the operator and took a long, deep breath.

"Operator. . . . How may I help you?"

"I want to call a phone number in Alberta, Canada," I said.

"What is the area code please?"

"I don't know."

"That's okay. I'll check for you. . . . The area code is 403. . . . What is the number you wish to call?"

I told her.

"That will be $5.75 for the first three minutes. Do you have the correct change?"

Nearly six dollars? Forget it. I had exactly six quarters, three dimes and four nickels in change.

"Uh, no. I don't have enough. I'll have to go get some."

"Very well. Call back when you have it."

I ran down the street for more change, then ran back to the phone booth and dialed the operator again. This time when she told me to deposit $5.75, I dropped in twenty-three quarters one after the other. That left me with seven quarters, three dimes and four nickels. . . . Not much if it took longer than three minutes to explain to Mom what was happening.

The phone rang and rang.

"There is no answer," the operator finally said. "Try calling later."

Later? Already I'd been gone ten minutes; I didn't have any later.

"Couldn't you just let it ring another few times?"

"I'll try again," the operator said. "But it won't do much good if nobody's home."

That was when it struck me that nobody *was* home. Mom was in Kelowna now for sure.

My quarters came rattling back a couple of minutes later. I tried to think who else I could use them to call but couldn't come up with anybody. With all the moves we'd made before the divorce, and Mom working shifts after the divorce, there weren't a whole lot of people we could call friends. The Edens, of course, but we'd passed them at the border. Jason's family, but they'd left for the lake two days before us.

I left the phone booth and went back to the car, where Paige was ready to skin me alive.

"You idiot. You could've gotten us all into awful trouble!"

"We are in awful trouble," I said.

"What's that supposed to mean?"

"I mean I don't think Dad plans to take us back home when this trip is over."

Paige didn't laugh like I expected her to. "Grow up, you dork, and get a brain."

"Look, you miserable brat," I said, grabbing her by the shoulders and shocking her into silence. "We're heading into Idaho. Now does that make sense? Dad told us he was taking us to the coast for our holidays."

Paige shrugged. "Let go of me. How do I know? Nothing makes much sense. I thought holidays were supposed to be fun. I can hardly wait for this one to be over."

"Well, what I'm trying to say is that it won't ever be over. Why do you suppose Dad didn't want the Edens to see us? Why do you suppose Grandma gave him money?"

"Dad's always broke," Cory said. "That's what Mom says."

"Sure," Paige said. "Grandma gave him money for him to take us on a holiday."

"Yeah? When we could have stayed with her for free?"

For once Paige looked doubtful.

"And," I said, "before we left home, Mom was talking to her lawyer about whether she had to let us go with Dad. It doesn't take a genius to figure out she was scared something like this might happen."

I stopped there because Cory's eyes were getting bigger and bigger.

"Suppose you're right," Paige said. "Suppose he doesn't plan to take us back. . . . He can't make us go with him. We're not helpless little kids."

"Maybe not, but I don't know what to do. Mom's not home."

My mind raced. No. It spun its wheels.

"Yeah, well," Paige said. "I think it's awful the way you're always making Dad out to be some kind of big mean monster. You get all stiff and scared-looking when he's around, and he doesn't know what to say to you. If you wouldn't act like that, he'd be able to talk to you and you'd see—"

"Oh, for heaven's sake. Would you quit babbling! I'm trying to think what to do."

"You sound just like him. I wish you'd quit acting like him and listen to me. Dad couldn't possibly be kidnapping us. How could he? How could he possibly keep his eye on us every minute of every day?"

"Maybe you're right," I admitted. "At least, it'd be hard once we're overdue and Mom reports us missing."

"Stop saying that," Paige said, hitting me. "Stop talking like that. You're crazy, Debbie, right off-the-wall loony tunes!"

"And how bad can it be?" I said automatically protecting my head with my arms. "If worse comes to worst, all we have to do is get out and start walking some time when he goes into a beer parlor."

Paige shut up when I said that, and I figured for sure that was the end of the topic till Dad did or said something to prove me either right or wrong. But I hadn't counted on Paige's knack for barging in noisily where I would have tiptoed.

"Hey, Dad," she called out from the back seat of the car later that day. "Just where are we going? Debbie says we're heading east. I thought you said we were going to the coast."

I saw Dad's grip on the steering wheel tighten, but his voice was very casual as he answered.

"I've changed my mind," he said. "We're going to Colorado. It'll be a lot more fun, don't you think?"

"Yeah, I guess. What's supposed to be fun about Colorado?"

"Well, uh . . . it's got mountains."

We'd already been through mountains—lots of mountains—but nobody was about to point that out.

"When do we get there?" Paige asked.

"Hey, this is a holiday, remember? We don't have to be on a schedule. I wouldn't be making this a very fun trip if I put us on a strict schedule."

Paige thought for a minute. "Let's send Mom a postcard," she suggested.

"Yeah, but she's not home."

"So what? It'll take awhile for the card to get there anyway."

"You'll be home before it arrives probably. I don't know, but it seems like a lot of work for nothing to me."

"Yeah? We'll be home before it can get there?" Paige gave me an I-told-you-so look. "So you're not kidnapping us, eh?"

Funny. Paige obviously thought it was a good joke until Dad pulled over to the side of the road and turned to face us.

"What makes you say a thing like that?" he asked.

Paige looked kind of embarrassed. "Well," she said, "Debbie thinks . . ."

Dad shifted his gaze to me. "Debbie thinks? Really? And just what is it that Debbie thinks?"

Even Paige was fast catching on to the fact that she had put her foot in it big time. She looked from Dad to me and started backing off.

"Oh, it was just a joke. . . ."

"Yeah? Well, tell me this joke so I can have a good laugh, too."

"Come to think of it, it wasn't that funny."

"You're very quiet, Deb," Dad said. "Suppose you tell me this funny joke."

I was quaking inside, but I decided to go for it, to clear the air once and for all.

"It was just a dumb joke about ending up on a milk carton," I said. "It wasn't anything."

"Yeah? Well, Deb, my girl, that was a very interesting joke. How would you feel about coming to live with me instead of going home to your mother?"

Dad glanced at each of us and said, "As bad as all that? Why? What's the matter with me?"

"Uh, nothing, Dad," I mumbled. "But—"

"I can give you everything your mom can give you." He bit his lip when we didn't say anything. "I can. I can give you more."

Cory looked strangely stiff. I figured I'd just found out where the expression scared stiff came from.

"A pony!" Dad grinned suddenly. "Just think of that. A pony. Where we're going—"

"Our very own pony?" Paige asked.

"The next thing to it. A pony that you can ride all the time and take care of just as if it was your very own. Which it will be. Practically."

"Why won't it be all our own? Why only practically our own?"

"Because I'm not made of money," Dad said through clenched teeth. He took a deep breath. "Hey, try to understand—I'm doing the best I can. Maybe it will be all your own soon. If I get a promotion someday. If you guys don't keep needing new shoes every four months—"

"You've got a job?" I blurted out.

"All arranged, right and tight. A friend of mine's hiring me."

"So you weren't planning on bringing us home," Paige said.

"I was planning on making you a new home," Dad replied.

"Mom's got custody," I pointed out.

"Maybe, but I've got you."

Obviously, I'd rubbed him on a sore spot. I'd wiped the grin right off his face.

He continued. "You guys don't care two hoots about me, do you?"

"Yes, we do." It was Cory, speaking up for the first time. "Really we do. We love you."

"We love you lots and lots," Paige added.

Right at that moment, I didn't feel I could love a bully like Dad. But when he waited for me to say I did and his eyes started to turn red because I wouldn't say it, I felt like a real snake.

"We'd miss Mom," Paige said. "It's not that we don't want to see you; it's just that we'd miss her something awful."

"Have you guys forgotten that you won't be seeing me once you move to Kelowna?"

"But you could move to Kelowna, too," I said.

"Why should I have to move in order to be with my kids?"

"But we've moved lots of times."

"This is different. She's moving to get away from me. I wouldn't give her the satisfaction of following her."

"Oh, it wouldn't give Mom satisfaction," Paige said. "She'd hate it."

"She'll hate this even more," Dad said softly.

Hate what? My mind ran wild. People had been known to shoot all their kids and then shoot themselves. For a minute I thought maybe that was what Dad was talking about.

But, no, it was only kidnapping that he had in mind. Only kidnapping.

Dad sat silent and still for what seemed like a very long time. Finally, he roused himself and looked straight at me. "You are coming to live with me," he said in a flat voice. "That's all there is to it. I suggest you get used to the idea."

He looked quickly at the others. "Yes," he said, "that's how it is. And one more thing. This is a dangerous and violent country. Kids go missing. Kids get stolen and sold—for what, I leave to your imaginations. Kids also get abused and murdered. You don't want to have to go it alone without me. You need me to keep you safe. 'Nuff said? Good. Now we understand each other."

He turned back to the wheel, put the car in gear and shoulder-checked for traffic, but he didn't pull away. "You know," he said in a low, husky voice, "it's not every divorced dad who loves his kids enough to risk everything to be with them. Lots of dads never even bother seeing their kids after a divorce."

Half an hour later, he pulled the car over again and took up where he'd left off, as though he'd never stopped talking. Only now there was a phony sound to his voice that was completely different from before. "I hope you know, Paige, that they'll put me in prison if you rat on me. They'll lock me up with the druggies and the killers."

Paige started sniffling, and I sat grinding my teeth because the twerp couldn't tell when Dad was being real and when he was being fake.

"And don't think," he said in a queer, hard voice as he turned to look at me, "that I won't know who I have to thank for it if I do wind up in jail.

As a threat, that sounded about as real as they come.

CHAPTER 4

DAD STARTED KEEPING CORY WITH HIM EVERY MINUTE OF the day and night. Cory was terrified that Paige and I would leave without him. As though I'd even think of it! I had just turned seven when he was born. I put away my dolls and adopted him for my very own.

The first time Paige and I were alone in a washroom, I said we now knew now for sure, and she sure had made it ten times harder to get away.

Paige backed me up against a sink. "Get away? Get real, Debbie. We don't have any money. We're a long way from home. What're we supposed to do—walk? How well do you know your geography? Do you know how to get home?"

"Yes," I said sharply. "I do know my geography. I can get us home. But we don't have to get home. . . . All we have to do is get to a police station. Heck, all we have to do is get to a phone so we can call a police station."

Paige stopped throwing a fit. "Yeah?"

"Of course."

"We turn Dad in to the police?"

What kind of daughter sends her father to jail? Well, I'd have to worry about that later. Even if I could have been sure that we'd end up back home in six months or a year, without taking any risks or doing anything, I still couldn't have stood the thought of spending a minute more than I had to living with Dad. It wasn't the way he forgot to feed us or the way he stomped on us every time we opened our mouths . . . well, it was, but it wasn't just that. It was wanting to be with Mom. I wanted it so badly that my chest ached.

If I felt that way, I was pretty sure that a kid as small as Cory had to be feeling even worse. And when we didn't show up as expected, Mom would worry herself sick until we made it home again.

"But what if the police don't believe us," Paige said. "What if they believe Dad instead?"

"They'll believe us," I said grimly.

"But what if they don't?"

"Oh, stuff a sock in it, Paige."

"It's easier for a grownup to get people to listen to them," Paige said.

"Well, I'm going to act super grown up myself."

"He'll probably say we're just mad at him—"

"He'll probably say," I corrected her, "that Mom has been filling our heads with garbage about him. That's what Mom thinks anyway. I'll figure out a way of fixing that. That's not what worries me."

What worried me was I was sure we'd have only one crack at getting away. If we blew it . . .

I watched for the sort of opportunities we could take advantage of. But since Cory was kind of Dad's hostage, getting away with him seemed ten times more impossible than getting away without him. Even at night, we couldn't sneak away because Dad slept with Cory and kept one arm up against him all the time. I know. That first night after we came to "understand" each other, I woke up five or six times and looked over at the bed where Dad and

Cory were sleeping. Dad woke up if Cory even so much as twitched in his sleep.

But still, there had to be times when a man would slip up a bit in his watchfulness. If we were ready to act the minute Dad slipped up, we'd be away before he knew what hit him.

In the heavily wooded, hilly country of Idaho, Dad did slip up. We pulled into a self-serve gas station along the highway to fill up. When it came time for Dad to go pay the cashier, Cory was asleep in the front seat. Dad hesitated and then went alone to pay for the gas.

"This is it," I said to Paige. "If we make a run for it now, we stand a good chance of getting away."

I started to shake Cory.

"C'mon, Cory, wake up. Quick. We can make a run for it!"

Cory groaned in his sleep and tried to shrug away from my hand. Paige threw a fit of hysterics.

"Are you crazy, Debbie? It'll never work. We'll never get away."

By the time Cory woke up and Paige calmed down, Dad had already paid the cashier and was starting to turn away from the wicket.

"Arghh," I groaned. "Why were you so slow?"

Paige was darting quick little glances at Dad and at the woods. I could tell that in spite of what she had just been saying she was measuring the distance and her chances of making it to the woods before Dad caught her.

I put my hand on her arm. "Forget it, Paige. It's too late now. We'll have to wait for another chance. We'll have to be quicker, that's all. And when we do make a run for it, we'll do it together. Understand?"

"We need a code word," Paige said. "So we know right away that it's time, and we don't even think about it."

We thought about that as we drove on that day, and Paige eventually came up with "oops." I figured it was a pretty good code word. For one thing, you didn't say it very often—like maybe once in ten years, unless you happened to be Mom—and you could say it in a tone of voice that got people's attention, without sounding desperate or dramatic. It was short. It was easy to remember. And it was something that reminded us of Mom. After all, getting home to Mom was what this whole thing was about. So "oops" it was. I warned Cory and Paige that they'd better leave it to me to say it but that we'd all have to be ready to jump no matter who said it.

It looked as though we wouldn't have to use our code word when our very next stay at a motel brought our landlady around to see why we weren't getting any hot water. She was a friendly person with steel-gray hair and small, curious eyes—and she was curious about us.

"Wouldn't you children rather be outside playing?" she asked, looking at how we sat in a row on the couch watching her work with her pliers and wrench.

Dad dropped a frying pan lid with a clatter and came over to stand near the couch.

"I wouldn't want them playing outside in a strange town," he said. "How much longer do you think you'll be?"

"Oh, we're no stranger than any other town," she replied, with a twinkle. "I'm sure they'd be quite safe."

"I'm not just being an over-protective parent," Dad said with a sad little smile. "I wouldn't be able to stand it if anything happened to these kids, and I'm afraid something could. The younger ones are too young to be responsible for the twelve-year-old, and her behavior can, at times, be right off the wall."

"Oh, I see." The woman stopped wrestling with the pipe long enough to shoot me a shrewd, appraising look.

Dad was also watching, so I had so sit there looking blank.

The woman didn't say anything as she put all her energy into tugging hard on her wrench. When it finally moved a few centimeters, she turned back to me with a smile. "You're twelve? You should help your father out. You're lucky to have one who takes you on trips."

Dad gave me a smug look of triumph.

"Perhaps I could rustle up a neighbor kid to take them to the playground."

"Thanks, but I just wouldn't feel easy. We've suffered one crushing loss already—we don't even know where their mother is right now . . . and . . . well, you know how it is."

"It's tough. Well, I wish you all the luck in the world. At least you'll have hot water tonight."

Dad thanked her all the way across the room and out the door.

He looked at us and his grin turned to a frown. "Oh, for pete's sake! Lighten up. I've got a treat in store for you. Tomorrow, I'm going to take you to see the Lewis and Clark Caverns."

But the little old lady wasn't through with Dad yet. She came back while we were eating supper, and she had an embarrassed-looking state trooper in tow.

"So sorry to disturb you. Clyde was just in checking our register, and he has one or two questions he wanted to put to you folks. I told him I was sure you wouldn't mind."

Clyde looked as though he minded, but he stepped forward to do his duty anyway.

"If I could just see your I.D. and the I.D. for the kids."

"Sure," Dad said in a super-hearty voice. He dug into his pocket for his wallet. "It was just a couple of days ago I was showing these at the border," he remarked mildly.

"Yeah, I know," the trooper said.

Dad gave him a sharp look, and he turned a dull shade of red. "It's not anything against you, Mr. Adaskin. It's just that—"

He stopped short of saying whatever he had been about to say, and he turned a kind of plum color. Dad looked quickly over at the motel lady.

"Hey, if anyone here has any doubts at all that I'm their father, I'm only too happy to set the record straight."

"Oh, that's not the issue here," the state trooper said. "Your wife not along on this trip, Mr. Adaskin?"

"No, we're divorced. Look, what's this about? Surely a man can take his kids on a holiday without everyone assuming he's a white slaver or something."

"You'd think he could, but Grace here is tender-hearted and sees abused kids under every rock, so to speak." He shrugged. "I'm sure you wouldn't want us to turn a blind eye if some kid was in trouble."

"Oh," Dad said, "I see. Well, of course, I understand. God knows, we have to look out for the kids."

The trooper was so relieved Dad was being understanding that he warmed right up to him. He rolled his eyes. "So, hey, just to set everyone's mind at ease, you won't mind if I talk to the kids for a minute or two."

"Of course not!"

The trooper looked pointedly at the door, and Dad

said, "I'll even leave the room." He turned to us. "Now, kids, you've got nothing to be afraid of. This policeman is only after bad people. He won't hurt you; he only hurts people who do bad things." And, with a long, backward look—especially at Paige and Cory—Dad went out.

The state trooper walked toward us, his leather boots and holster creaking mightily and his right hand resting unconsciously on his gun. Cory's eyes grew wide, and he began to cry.

"Hey, what's the matter?" the trooper asked, squatting in front of him.

"Please don't hurt my daddy," Cory begged.

"Hurt your daddy? No, of course I won't hurt your daddy. Your daddy doesn't, uh, hurt you does he?"

"Course not!"

"Do you live with your Daddy?" the trooper asked Paige.

"Well," Paige said, "we were living with our Mom, but—"

I figured it was time to step in.

"Mom has custody," I said. "Sole custody."

At the edge of the window, I caught a glimpse of a shadow. Dad eavesdropping . . . Well, he couldn't hurt me if I did this right. All I had to do was sound reasonable, very, very reasonable. And mature.

"Not that there's anything wrong with Dad," I said. "But Mom does have custody. We should be living with her."

"So your dad is an okay guy, is he?"

"Oh, yes!" I stressed that. No way Dad was going to come back into the room and convince everybody that Mom had poisoned my mind against him. "Dad's okay."

The motel lady spoke up then. "I tell you, Clyde, it

wasn't natural the way they were just sitting there all in a row. What kids would sit like that after a day of driving? Kids who are kept on a mighty tight leash, I tell you."

"A tight leash isn't abuse, Grace."

"They're scared of him."

"Are you scared of your daddy?"

At the moment, Paige and Cory looked more scared of the state trooper.

Grace came over and hunkered down in front of us like the trooper had. "You don't have to be scared of your daddy, you know," she said. "I personally guarantee you they'll lock him up and throw away the key if he's done anything to—"

"No!" Paige cried. "I don't want him to go to jail!"

"But you do want to live with Mom," I said.

Paige looked at me like I was talking French.

"Mom. You want to live with Mom."

"Oh, yeah, of course."

The trooper turned to me. "And you say it's your mom who's the legal guardian."

"Oh, yes!"

"Well . . ." He stood up slowly like he had so much muscle that it made it hard for him to move.

The shadow at the window was gone in a flash.

"Mr. Adaskin! If you could just come in here, sir."

Dad came in smiling.

"Could you tell me who has custody of these three children, sir?"

"Why, I do!"

"You do?"

"Yes, of course!"

"You have papers to prove that, I suppose?"

"Well, yes I do."

Dad walked over to his suitcase with more calm than you'd expect, seeing that he was just about to find himself in big trouble. I held my breath, waiting to see what he was going to do next. Not make a run for it and get shot in the back, I hoped. No, not that. Probably hunt and hunt and then say he'd lost the papers.

Dad rummaged around in his suitcase, and the state trooper creaked as he shifted impatiently.

"Ah, here they are," Dad said, finally holding up a couple of long sheets of paper.

The trooper looked them over.

Dad looked at me with absolutely glittering eyes. An awful suspicion began to grow in me that Dad was actually going to manage somehow to pull this thing off. The longer the trooper read, the closer to my ankles my stomach dropped.

"Hmm. These are photocopies. Do you have originals?"

"Are you kidding? In Canada, we aren't given originals!"

The trooper read the papers through a second time, slowly, and then came over to me and hunkered down. "Here," he said, "I want to show you something so you'll understand."

I dragged my eyes down to the paper he held out in front of me, but I couldn't make any sense of it. Two words in large, bold type, however, caught my eye: "CUSTODY AGREEMENT."

"Your dad does have custody. See?" He put a finger the size of a sausage where it said "sole custody" and my dad's name. Then he ran his finger down to where it said "reasonable access" and my mom's name. "What made you think your mom had custody?"

"I—I—"

"Give her time to think," Grace said. "She's just twelve."

For an awful moment, I thought maybe Dad did have custody.

"Well?"

"I, uh, we were living with Mom."

"Of course, you were, Deb," Dad said soothingly. "Until I could get settled and arrange a place for you. You surely didn't think you were going to Kelowna with her did you?"

"I . . . yes. Yes we were. I mean, we are."

Dad shook his head sadly. "Gosh, Deb, I'm sorry. You know I am. . . . You know I wish you could if that's what you really want. But we have to face facts here."

The trooper ran a big, beefy hand through his hair. "The kids didn't know who had custody?"

"Oh, yes, they did. Well, maybe the other two are too young to understand, but Debbie knows. Don't think just because I'm gentle with her that she doesn't know. You know perfectly well, don't you, Deb?"

My throat tightened up, and my mouth wouldn't work right, but I got it out. "I know who has custody. Mom does."

Dad looked at me for about a minute, then shook his head.

"Okay," he said, "you say Mom has custody? You say that's what you believe? Well, I hate to show my own daughter up as a liar, but I guess I'll have to, won't I?"

I stared after him as he turned and got something else out of his suitcase . . . another sheet of paper. This one was small and crumpled.

He handed it to the state trooper. "It's her handwriting, as you'll have no difficulty verifying."

The state trooper scanned the sheet, and then read it through slowly. When he was finished, he turned to look accusingly at me. Without a word, he handed the sheet to Grace. She read it, then looked at me a whole lot like the trooper had.

"What? What is it?"

Grace handed it to me, the letter I had started to write to Mom that first night outside Rocky Mountain House. Lord, I'd never thought of it again, never even seen it again. Now the words did a little dance before my eyes: "I don't care what the courts say, nobody should've made me go with him. Let the little kids go with him . . . they wanted to, but I should be with you." Only Dad would look at me now. The other two seemed to find me embarrassing.

"It doesn't mean what you think it means," I said, but they were done listening to me.

"Well, you were wise to carry your papers with you," the trooper said to Dad.

"I almost didn't because we are just on vacation. But, well, you know, you hear about this kind of thing. I'd hate anybody to think I was kidnapping my own kids."

The trooper sighed. "I only wish more people had your good sense. It'd make my job a heck of a lot easier." He turned to Grace, and his tone of voice changed. "I only hope that'll be a lesson to you, Grace," he said. "I'm thinkin' you spoiled those kids of yours pretty darn bad, and that's a shame, but it's nothin' to harassin' every poor soul you hear lose their temper in a mall or see leavin' kids waitin' in a hot car. You do stretch a man's patience sometimes!"

Dad saw them out and then turned to us. "You ought to become a lawyer," he said to me. "'Mom's got custody.

Mom's got custody.' You never think how she may have
custody, but I'm the one who loves you enough to take all
sorts of risks to have you with me. I hope to God that
someday you appreciate that more. Well, hell, I know
that some day you're going to appreciate that and thank
me for what I've done. Anyway, it's water under the
bridge, right? I mean, it wasn't you who called the police,
right? Tomorrow, we'll go see the Lewis and Clark Caverns, and you'll see that you're really very lucky to be
with me."

CHAPTER 5

THE MINUTE WE STEPPED INSIDE THE HUGE CAVE SYSTEM, I knew the situation had possibilities. We were part of a tour group and that meant part of a crowd. And that meant it was easy to get separated from Dad. In fact, in some narrow passages, we had to go single file.

Dad didn't seem particularly worried about losing us. Maybe he figured we wouldn't try anything now that we knew he had custody papers that looked real enough to fool the authorities. Or maybe it just never crossed his mind that we'd try to bolt in a huge maze of caves that were deep underground and pitch dark without the tour guide's lights.

But scary as it would be, I knew it could work. All we had to do was get left behind, slip down a side passage and hide behind a boulder. When they began to search for us, they would expect us to want to be found. They would shout a lot but not look too closely. Even if Dad suspected we were hiding, he would probably not tell anybody that.

It would mean waiting in the dark for a while, maybe even overnight. But eventually we would follow the lights of a tour group out toward the exit. When the coast was clear, we'd slip out through the exit and cut across country home to Mom.

The entrance and exit were half a mile apart. It was farther than that from the ticket booth and parking lot. The setup was perfect. We'd never get as good a chance as this again. The only problem was I'd forgotten that both Cory and Paige had a deep and abiding fear of the dark. When I said "oops," they both looked at me with such shocked disbelief that my heart sank.

I rolled my eyes and jerked my head over my shoulder, but a stubborn "no" was already settling into place on their faces.

"It'll be okay," I whispered. "We'll follow the next tour group out to the mouth of the cave."

But they both stood there frozen, wasting precious time. I tried making the sort of faces that mothers do when they want to bawl out their kids in church without actually saying anything, but it was plain to see that neither Paige nor Cory cared two hoots about being bawled out by me.

"You go ahead," Paige hissed. "Good luck. As for Cory and me, we'd rather stick with Dad than try that." They turned their backs on me and started walking slowly after the others.

I was mad enough to kick stalagmites. But there wasn't anything I could do about it, so I hurried after them and tried to stop looking like someone who'd just eaten a toad. There would be other chances. Surely, there would be other chances.

Going to the Lewis and Clark Caverns kind of made our trip feel like more of a holiday. Dad seemed to expect that we would forget Mom now that we were doing holiday sorts of things. In fact, he lightened up and got very cheerful and chummy as we were leaving the caves.

"Hey, look," Dad said, pointing to a sign along the

highway a couple of hours later. "We're coming to Earthquake Lake. You'll be able to see a real honest-to-goodness fault line and a lake that was tipped on its ear by an earthquake. Interested?"

"Sure. I guess so," Paige said without much enthusiasm.

Cory didn't know what a fault line was, so he couldn't be expected to say much. I hadn't said ten words since the caves, and I wasn't about to start at that point.

Dad turned and looked at us all. "What's the matter with you? You're a hell of a bunch of wet blankets."

We didn't know what to say to that either, so we shifted uncomfortably in our seats and said nothing.

"What is it?" he asked. "Too lazy to want to learn something new outside of school? Maybe you think we should be spending our whole time in video arcades and watching stupid shows on motel TV sets?"

He was working himself into a temper. I could see the signs, but I didn't know what to do about it.

"Kids these days!" Dad snorted with disgust. "You know the trouble with you?"

Uh-oh. For sure Dad was going to tell us just what was wrong with us . . . probably in great detail and at great length.

"Well?"

Well, what? Did he expect an answer? Paige and I looked quickly at each other, but neither of us knew what to say.

Dad smacked the dashboard with the palm of his hand. The noise made us all jump, especially Cory, who was closest to him. "Are you listening to me?"

"Yes." We all said it at once.

"Good."

He drove along not saying anything more, and I began to wonder if that was the end of the lecture. I was also wondering if Dad was maybe just a bit bonkers. I mean, what kind of guy stops lecturing you the minute you say you're listening? For that matter, what kind of guy goes around smacking things with his hand so he can startle other people and make them jump? I just hoped he wasn't crazy enough to do anything really drastic.

Like kidnap us maybe?

"Wipe that smirk off your face," Dad ordered.

My face must have shown something of what I was thinking. As luck would have it, Dad had been looking in the rearview mirror.

"You know, Deb," Dad said in a voice like scalding acid, "you really are stupid. I know you think you're smart—and maybe you get pretty good marks at school— but you're still basically Stupidity with Zits. You know why?"

I didn't dare not answer this time. "Why?"

"Don't talk back!" he screamed.

"But—"

I really was Stupidity with Zits. Had I really started to argue that I thought he wanted an answer?

"But what?"

"Nothing."

Dad said something I wouldn't repeat even if I could and made a U-turn right in the middle of the highway.

"You made me miss the turnoff!"

He took to swearing instead of lecturing, and we all sat paralyzed and staring straight ahead, waiting for the torrent of words to end.

Dad pulled into a parking lot at an interpretive center. Still boiling over with anger, he roared across it at eighty clicks an hour and headed toward a spot high above the lake with no guard rail.

As we all knew, there was nothing about that old car that could be depended on—least of all the brakes. We all pressed our feet hard against the floor.

The car stopped in a dry skid at the very edge of the steep drop-off, and we all sat there for a minute, sweating quietly. Even Dad seemed to have vented all his anger. He became very subdued.

Then he turned to me and said very, very quietly, "In future, don't get smart with me, Deb, or so help me God . . ."

I finished the sentence for him a hundred different ways as we walked through the interpretive center, looking at pictures and reading what was written beneath them.

I don't remember a single thing we saw. I didn't understand a single word we read. I walked on legs that trembled. I unconsciously scratched till blood trickled down my arms. I looked blindly where Dad pointed, with eyes that wouldn't even focus.

I tried to pull myself together. It wasn't the end of the world, just another one of Dad's temper tantrums.

Just? Temper tantrums aren't scary in a two-year-old, but in a thirty-two-year-old . . .

We left Earthquake Lake and drove up the road to where a scar in the earth was plainly visible. This, Dad said with a return of enthusiasm, was a fault line. This was where the earth had moved, going different directions along this line. Today, you could step over the line, no problem. Back in 1955, though, when the earth had quaked, this would have been a terrifying place to be. Weren't the forces of nature awesome?

We obediently stepped back and forth across the line and agreed that the forces of nature were awesome.

The fault line ran through a very pretty campground. Dad liked it so much that he decided we should spend the night. Of course, we still had only two blankets, but it was a hot day and Dad was sure it was going to be a warm night—a lot warmer than in the high country west of Rocky Mountain House.

We didn't have any food with us except for four chocolate bars, but Dad didn't figure that'd be any problem either because we'd eaten about three o'clock in the afternoon.

"You'll be fine until morning," he told us.

The smell of hamburgers frying in a pan full of onions drifted over from a nearby campsite. We looked at each other but didn't say anything.

"C'mon," Dad said, "let's build a fire. How long has it been since you've had a campfire?"

We gathered firewood, and Dad worked hard at getting a fire going. It wasn't easy because he didn't have any paper with him or an ax to chop the wood into smaller pieces. I'll never understand how forest fires get started—Dad worked carefully, piling up a thrown-away brown paper bag and some dried pine needles and twigs in the middle of a tepee made of the smallest sticks he could find, but still his little fire smoked and died as soon as the flames hit the sticks.

That meant we had to search out more dried needles and twigs and try to find more paper that could be used as kindling. That wasn't easy.

Cory was the one who came up with the idea of using some sheets of outhouse toilet paper. Dad got fire number two started and huddled over it, fanning it gently and praying it into life. But that one fizzled, too, so we were sent out to scrounge up more stuff to burn. Dad pulled apart the charred sticks so he could build his little nest in the middle again.

He was so intent on what he was doing that, for once, he'd forgotten us. I stood on a little hill at the edge of the campground, pulling grandfather's beard off a tree, when suddenly I looked back and realized that Cory was over behind the woodpile and Paige was picking up wood shavings in an empty campsite on the far side of the campground. We were all a long way away from Dad, and he hadn't even noticed. The time was perfect for us to slip quietly into the woods, but how was I supposed to let the others know? They were too far away for me to signal to them without signaling to Dad, too. If only they would look at me!

But they didn't. I started to scramble down the bank to go get them, but at that very moment, a big red-haired man came over to Dad with a hatchet and an armful of newspapers and asked if he would like to borrow them to get his fire started.

Dad thanked the man and accepted the loan. And with the fire now a sure thing, he suddenly thought of us, looked quickly around and called us back to the campsite.

Another perfect chance was gone. We sat around the fire, eating our chocolate bars and drinking water while the families in the campsites near us ate burgers and toasted marshmallows around their campfires.

"Quit watching the neighbors," Dad ordered at one point. "You look so pitiful. What's the matter with you? Why can't you enjoy yourselves? I swear, you're the most pathetic excuse for kids I've ever had the misfortune of spending time with!"

We tore our eyes away from the neighbors, though at the moment, the kids were riding the red-haired man's legs and he was clumping around pretending to be a monster or a giant.

"Sing," Dad ordered.

We stared at him.

"Sing. You guys must know some campfire songs. Well, sing them."

Paige started to sing the song she'd done as a solo at the Christmas concert. Her voice rose through the night as though a little, lost angel was sending a message home: "If religion was a thing that money could buy, the rich would live and the poor would die . . . all my trials, Lord, soon be over."

My throat got tight and sore. The other campers stopped horsing around and listened to her clear, high, sweet voice. Dad put his head in his hands and stared at the fire. When the last quavering notes died out, no one moved or said anything, and Dad didn't suggest we sing anymore.

I sat and let the fire hypnotize me. Three chances we'd had to get away, and we'd missed every one of them. We simply couldn't afford to miss another one. But the more I thought of it, the less I liked making a dash for it without some kind of head start. Cory was simply too little to run far enough and fast enough to get away if Dad was right on our tail. We needed something to give us a few minutes head start.

Impossible.

No, not quite impossible. What if Cory hid, and Dad took off looking for him? While Dad was gone, we could all disappear. We might have five minutes or more in which to do it. Of course, it would have to be Cory who hid because if anybody else did it, Dad would take Cory with him to look for them. Luckily, chances were good he wouldn't bother dragging Paige and me along if it was Cory he was looking for. He seemed to realize that we wouldn't go anywhere without Cory.

Okay, but where would we hide Cory? Did we have to count on spotting a good hiding place when the time came?

I didn't like having to leave things to chance like that. And I didn't like the pressure of having to think fast or hide Cory while in a panic. Still, what choice did I have?

Paige moved over closer to me, and I put my arm around her. What a skinny little kid she was!

Suddenly, I had a thought. There was room for Cory in the trunk of the car. Dad would never dream that Cory might be hiding there. It was perfect.

I told Paige about the plan later at the outhouse.

"I thought you were smart, Debbie," she said. "But here you are still talking about running away. I suppose you think we're going to walk home."

"I am smart," I said. "I can get us home walking."

"What about those people who hurt little kids?"

"That was mainly Dad trying to scare us. You see, he knows just like I do that we can get home without him."

"Maybe it wouldn't be so bad being with Dad."

"Are you kidding?"

"Well, what if Dad takes the car keys with him?"

"No problem," I reassured her. "We don't need the keys. We can get into the trunk by taking off the back seat. Remember how Dad did that when he brought home the lumber for the bunk beds he was going to make us?"

"Maybe Dad did it, but do you know how to do it?"

"Sure. You just lift. That's all."

"You're sure you're strong enough?"

"Of course I'm sure," I said. I wasn't really. Still, how heavy could a back seat be? And if that back seat had to be lifted so we could get away, well then I'd lift it no matter what it took.

Paige went into the outhouse first, and her voice came small and childish out of the dark. "I hope there aren't any spiders in here. Hey, Debbie, what if Dad does take us with him?"

"He won't."

"But what if he does?"

"Well, then, we'll just have to get away and run in opposite directions. We'll meet back where we started from after dark."

"Ooo."

I gathered Paige didn't like my idea.

"Okay," I said, thinking fast. "How about this? When we've gone a ways, you pretend to twist your ankle. If you can't go on and you're scared of being left alone, he'll have to let me stay with you."

"Hey, I like that idea," Paige said.

If there had been an award for the best imaginary case of the flu, Paige would have won it when she was eight. She also did great pretend tears and injuries—I know, because I got blamed for some of them.

So Paige was willing to give my new idea a try. That was more than half the battle. I was sure Cory wouldn't be a problem.

We slept pretty well that night, considering that I was excited and the back seat was uncomfortable. In the morning, we had a huge breakfast at a little diner and then drove into Yellowstone National Park.

The stark, black skeletons of thousands of trees from the 1988 forest fire made the landscape look awfully grim, and the sulfur pools that steamed in the middle of that bleakness looked so weird that I'd have believed it if someone told me the entrance to hell was just over the next hill.

Cory was plainly scared by it all—so much steam, such a stink and those heavy layers of crystals coating the dying and dead trees. He didn't want to go near the bubbling mud.

"Sissy," Dad teased. "Whatcha scared of, scaredy cat?"

Cory hung tightly onto my hand and looked down at Dad's sneakers.

Dad gave Cory a little shove. "Well, what are you scared of? Do you think I'm going to throw you into a boiling pool and scald all the skin off you till you look like a peeled grape?"

Cory hung on tighter.

Dad sighed. "Aw c'mon, Cory. My main man . . ."

Cory pressed up a little closer to me. Suddenly, Dad lost his temper.

"A-ha, you've guessed," he yelled in a terrifying voice. "That is why I brought you here—to cook you for dinner. Nice, plump, stewed little boy . . ."

He swooped down on Cory, grabbed him and swung him into the air in spite of the death grip Cory had on me.

"Off to the cooking pot," he yelled. "And if Debbie doesn't let go, she'll go into it, too."

I knew it was possible for him to be mad and still be joking. I'd seen it happen before, when Dad had said awful things to tease us because he was angry. But Cory really thought he was going to be thrown into the boiling water. He let out a shriek that could have peeled paint off a house. It threw Dad off balance, and he teetered dangerously for a moment before setting Cory down. Heads that had turned our way turned away again. Cory ran to me and threw his arms around my waist. Dad blushed fiery red and gave a half-hearted laugh.

"Hey, Cory. Can't you take a joke? God . . ."

Dad turned and walked away.

I bent over. "It's okay, Cory. Now stop crying and listen to me because I don't know when I'll get another chance like this to talk to you."

Dad stood about twenty meters from us, looking so alone and lonely that I almost felt sorry for him.

"Are you listening, Cory?" I felt his head nod against my stomach. "Okay. Next time Dad takes his eye off us for four or five minutes, we're going to put you in the trunk of the car and tell Dad you ran away." And he'll believe it after this, I thought.

"When he's run off to look for you, we'll get you out of the trunk and run away in the opposite direction. Got that? Trust me. Paige and I have worked it all out. We know what we're doing, and we know it'll work."

Our chance came later that same day at a little self-serve gas station on the other side of Yellowstone. Cory had been huddled kind of quietly in his seat ever since the hot springs. When he saw that we were pulling in for gas, he simply closed his eyes and looked very convincingly asleep. I hadn't told him to do that; he had thought of it all on his own.

Dad filled the tank, looked in and saw Cory sleeping, then walked over to pay the cashier. Just then a big bread truck pulled in, blocking us from Dad's view. We could wait a hundred years and still never have as good a setup as this.

"Oops," I said, and Cory opened his eyes and grinned at me.

"Get the keys," I said, already opening the back door. I jumped out and ran around to the back. Cory handed me the keys, and with trembling hands, I tried two in the lock before finding one that would turn.

"Quick! Inside!"

Cory dove into the trunk and started pushing his way toward the back, away from the hatch.

"You'll be okay?" I asked with sudden doubt.

Now that the trunk was about to close, Cory didn't look so sure, but he gulped and nodded so I shut it with a quiet click. I ran back to jam whatever key seemed to fit back into the ignition. Then I jumped into my seat, pulling the door shut as quietly as I could.

Paige sat there looking at me with big, wide, blue eyes set in a face as white as chalk. Seeing her look that scared gave me a jolt. Suddenly, I felt dizzy and saw spots before my eyes.

"Oh, Paige . . ."

I was going to say "What have we done?" but just then Dad came back. I bit the sentence off and sat watching him, waiting for him to notice that Cory was gone.

"What is it?" He had noticed our faces before noticing the empty front seat. "Hey . . ."

Now he had noticed that Cory was gone.

I swallowed hard and waited for him to ask his question.

"Where's Cory?"

"He went to the bathroom," Paige said.

Dad looked from her to me and back again.

"He said he had to even if it made you mad. . . ."

"So why did you let him?"

"It all happened so fast," I said. "I thought he was asleep."

"Why didn't you go with him?"

"We thought you wouldn't mind as much if we stayed here," Paige said, "but I do have to go, too."

"Why are you looking like you've just seen a ghost?"

Dad was, strangely enough, not so much angry as puzzled.

"Because," Paige said simply, "we knew you wouldn't like Cory going off like that . . . or us letting him."

"It was a dumb thing to do . . ." he started.

"I know," I said.

Dad sighed. He looked tired. Tired of the watching, of the hassle and the hard feelings. Looking at him, I wondered if there was something I could say that would make him take us home right then and there.

"I want to go home," I said.

Paige turned to stare at me and Dad stiffened. It didn't take a genius to figure out that "I want to go home" wasn't the magic phrase to get us there. But Dad didn't go off in a blaze of anger like he would have earlier that day.

"Aw, Deb, give it a rest for just five minutes!" He got in the car and moved it away from the pumps. "What's taking Cory so long?"

He got out of the car and went to check the washroom. He took the keys with him. Paige and I turned and started trying to lift the upper part of the back seat.

In less than a minute, Dad was back.

"He's not there!"

"Are you sure? Maybe he's just not answering the door," I said.

"The key is hanging on a nail right beside the cash register. I saw it just now as I went by. I don't think he ever did go to the washroom."

"Where could he have gone?" Paige asked in a dry whisper that sent chills up and down my spine, even though I knew exactly where Cory was.

"C'mon," Dad said. "We're going to go looking for him."

I couldn't believe our bad luck. After starting so well, everything that could have gone wrong had now gone wrong. Dad had taken the keys out of the ignition, and he was taking Paige and me with him to go look for Cory. This was going to be tougher than I had thought.

What scared me most, though, was something I didn't want to have to admit to Paige ever: we had tried to lift the back seat and it hadn't budged. Not even a little.

CHAPTER 6

DAD DID A QUICK SURVEY OF THE BACK OF THE SERVICE station. There was a little dump full of rusting machine parts and tin cans, a cleared space with a septic tank in the middle and a pile of old lumber. Back of that was a solid wall of dark pines and scrub poplar with only one path leading into it.

"Did you see which way he went?" Dad grabbed my shoulder and his hand felt more like a claw than a hand.

"No," I said.

He looked at me closely. "There are bears in the woods around here, you know."

"I didn't see which way he went," I insisted.

"No," he said, softly. "You wouldn't." He wet his lips. "I hope to God we find him before something happens to him."

The woods were thick and shadowy. I thought about how scared Cory would have been if he'd had to be alone in them, and I was glad he was in the trunk of the car. Unless, of course, he was scared there. Or trapped.

Dad headed off down the path into the woods, and Paige and I hurried along after him. Although he started off at an easy jog, he was soon flying low over the uneven ground. The deeper we went into the woods, the scareder he seemed to get and the faster he ran. Soon, we couldn't keep up with him anymore.

"Hurry," he shouted over his shoulder.

"I can't," Paige called. "I can't run any faster."

Dad swore as he stood there waiting for us to catch up. "I've never seen such a pair of useless turds."

We ran full tilt up a hill and found several paths we could take. I doubled over, holding a stitch in my side, while Dad surveyed the options and made his choice. Before I could straighten up, he was off and running again.

A couple of minutes later, a loud crash and a louder shout made Paige stop so suddenly that I bumped into her. Dad had disappeared where the side of a ravine had suddenly become very steep. From what we could see as we peered over the edge, he must have lost his footing and skidded down the hill. He was lying flat on his back in a tangle of little bushes near the bottom.

"Are you all right, Dad?" Paige called out.

Dad swore long and loudly.

"He's okay," I said. "Let's get out of here."

Backtracking, we saw nothing familiar. When we came to the place where the network of trails met, we didn't have any idea which one we should take to get back to the service station. Finally, we narrowed the possibilities down to two and took one. We figured it looked narrower than the others, and we remembered the path we'd been on as being really narrow.

As it turned out, we hadn't run very far when we came to a tree with a wildly twisted trunk.

"Uh-oh," Paige said. "I know I've never seen this before. I'd have remembered it."

"We can't go back. . . . What if we run into Dad?"

"We can't wander around looking for the service station either," Paige said. "What if Dad drives off with Cory in the trunk?"

That settled it. We started running back, though every breath I took was like sandpaper through my lungs.

Either Dad had made good time getting up out of the ravine, or we had wasted a lot of time getting lost. Whichever it was, we caught a glimpse of him through the trees just as we were turning into the trail back to the car.

"We've got to split up," I said.

Paige gave me a scared look, a lot like the one that had killed my escape plan in the cave.

"I'm sorry. . . . It's the only way."

"No."

"One of us has to get back to Cory while the other one leads Dad away."

"Why can't I go back to the car?"

"Can you lift the back seat?"

Without another word, Paige disappeared back down the trail with the twisted tree trunk. With Dad almost close enough to touch, I managed a burst of speed that surprised even me. But I didn't need it. Dad was going after Paige, not me.

Run, Paige, I prayed silently. Put everything you've got into it. You can do it. You've got to do it.

I said much the same sort of thing to myself as I wrestled with the back seat of the car a few minutes later. "Lift, Debra Ann Adaskin, you stupid witch. You got them into this. It's up to you to get them out. Lift."

The back seat went up, and Cory rolled out the bottom. In two minutes flat, I was pulling him by the arm into the bushes near the car. They were murder to try to break through, but I never felt a scratch as I yanked Cory through them to the clearer area beyond.

I was in a panic now that I had Cory with me. It was

all over for us if Dad ever got his hands on him. I was frantic to get him under cover while we still had the chance. But what cover was I supposed to get him under? What cover was good enough to hide him?

One thing was sure—since we'd separated, Dad would know we all had to come back to the service station eventually if we were going to get back together again. It was the most logical place to meet. The only place to meet. When he got tired of barging through the woods, he would think of that—of the ease of coming back to the starting point and just waiting and watching—and I wanted to be well hidden before he did that.

In the end, I chose a dry creek bed for our hiding place. By lying flat in it, we were, I thought, quite out of sight. In the dappled sunlight and shadows of early evening, I thought we would have been hard to see even close up, as long as we didn't move. In any case, I was counting on Dad not coming close. There didn't look to be any cover in the area, and I figured Dad would naturally tend to concentrate on places that looked good for hiding and ignore ones like the one where we were hiding.

At first, we lay there not doing much except panting and praying Dad away, but after a while, we calmed down and I realized we could feel vibrations in the ground every time a car pulled into or out of the service station. That reminded me of something we'd learned while studying Indians in grade five.

"Don't worry, Cory," I whispered. "We'll know if Dad's nearby. We'll feel vibrations in the ground."

"It's okay," Cory whispered back. "I'm not scared now."

It must be nice to be five years old and think your sisters know what they're doing. If I could have turned back time and gotten us back into the car at the moment the bread truck pulled in beside us, I'd have . . .

But what was the use? If I could have turned back time, I'd have turned it back to before we ever left on this horrible trip. In fact, I'd have turned it back to that night when I had woken up Paige with my scratching. Then, when she hit me, I'd have said, "Sorry, Paige, I didn't mean to wake you up."

I looked at Cory. He was lying on his stomach, and he'd put his head down on his arms. His long, dark eyelashes fluttered against the pale blue skin under his eyes, a shock of blond hair fell over one eyebrow and his dusty blue-jeaned legs stretched out in opposite directions.

Suddenly, he opened his big brown eyes. "I thought you were looking at me," he whispered. "How long do we have to stay here?"

"Till after dark."

"Where do you think Paige is?"

I shrugged. "Paige'll be okay."

She would be if she could outrun Dad—and that might be possible if he'd hurt something when he took that tumble down the side of the ravine. Even if she couldn't outrun him, maybe she'd be able to hide. If not . . . I didn't want to think about it.

"Will she be able to find us?" Cory whispered.

"Sure she will. Paige is a smart girl."

"Yeah," he smiled, totally reassured.

How smart was Paige? Smart enough to find her way back here even if she had to retrace her way along those forest paths or somehow figure out a new way back? Was she smart enough to figure out that Dad would be watching for us? And could she handle being in the woods in the dark?

Cory raised his head again. "I hope a bear doesn't eat her," he hissed.

"Shh."

We lay there about another hour when suddenly I heard a car's engine whine and reluctantly turn over, then roar into life. Clank. Clank. Clank.

"I'd know that sound anywhere," I whispered to Cory.

"What do you mean?"

"That's Dad. He's going."

Cory looked doubtful. "Would he just drive off and leave us?"

"I don't know. I hope so."

Cory gave me a funny look, and I was afraid he was going to burst into tears.

"One good thing," I whispered. "He can't have found Paige. I think we'd have heard some talking or something if he'd come back with Paige."

The car pulled out of the service station and went down the highway a short distance before it stopped. Cory and I listened and looked at each other.

"I guess he's just moved the car," I warned Cory.

"Why?"

"So we won't see it when we come back to meet each other."

"But we heard it. . . ."

"Yeah, but he doesn't know that."

"Oh." Cory thought for a while. "Does that mean he's going to start looking for us around here?"

"Maybe."

"I don't think this is such a great hiding place."

At that moment, I didn't think so either. I thought about crawling up the creek bed until we were much farther into the woods. But moving seemed riskier than lying still. And, besides, the evening shadows were beginning to darken and lengthen.

"It's a good hiding place," I assured Cory. "Just as long as we're very, very quiet."

Cory did up an imaginary zipper on his lip and put his head back down on his arms. It got dark before he spoke again.

"Paige doesn't like the dark," he whispered.

"I know."

"I hope she comes soon."

"Can you stay alone for a minute while I take a look around?"

"Do I have to?"

"It's for Paige. I want to find her if I can."

"How long will it take you?"

"Three minutes, max."

"Okay."

I duck-waddled away from the gully toward the back of the station and the point where the path came out of the woods. With my hands, I brushed the ground ahead of me so I wouldn't accidentally step on a twig or anything. I kept my head low, and stopped and listened every few meters.

No sign of Paige. No sign of Dad.

Undecided about what to do, I squatted and looked around. How long had I been away from Cory? Five minutes maybe? Could I go a little farther before I absolutely had to get back to him? I decided I could and began to edge forward again.

Suddenly, a car pulled into the service station, and its headlights raked the bush in a wide arc. I dropped to my knees and put my cheek to the ground, shaken to my very bones.

Only a few meters ahead of me, the headlights had reflected off a grimacing white face: Dad, blinded by the sudden light in his eyes. Dad, sitting very still under a spruce tree.

I went back to Cory on my hands and knees.

"You were gone hours," he accused.

"Shh. I saw Dad."

"What about Paige?"

"No. No sign of Paige."

"What do we do now?"

How was I supposed to know?

Cory kneed me in the ribs. "Hey, Debbie. What're we supposed to do now?"

"Shh. I'm thinking."

After a bit, a few things became clearer to me. One of them was that we had to find Paige. We couldn't just leave her to spend a night alone in the woods. Another was that we had to stop her from walking right into Dad's arms.

What if she was, even now, making her way up the highway toward the service station? What if the trail had come out on the highway and she'd started back up it?

That was a chance we'd just have to take. Our best chance of finding Paige was to go where she had been seen last.

"Okay, Cory. I've figured it out." I groped with my hand till I found his head, then put my lips right up to his ear. "Chances are Paige is back in the woods. This dry creek bed will takes us back there, around Dad and right to where we want to go. It's a perfect road, except that we don't want to make any noise, and the stones could make quite a racket if we're not careful. So, Cory, we've got to go very quietly along the creek bed. Do you think you can do it?"

"Course I can."

"Good for you! Let's go."

We wormed our way slowly through the shadows, over the gravel and big chunks of rock that lined our highway into the woods. We went silently in single file and eventually reached the path I was looking for.

"Okay, this is it. We should be safe now."

We stood up and stretched our backs with a sigh of relief. Then I pointed Cory in the right direction, and we started picking our way along the narrow trail. It wasn't exactly my idea of a good time. Cory held on tightly to my hand. My heart was thudding.

"Oops . . . oops . . . oops . . ."

The words were so faint, I thought I was imagining them. Then Cory heard them, too.

"What's that?"

"Oops."

Then dead silence.

We took a few more steps, peering anxiously into the dark shadows ahead. Suddenly, Cory squeezed my hand hard.

There, a few meters ahead of us, Paige sat with her arms around her knees.

"I knew you'd come for me," she said happily. "What took you so long?"

Cory ran to hug Paige.

"Boy, am I ever glad to see you!"

"What were you doing sitting there?" I asked. I didn't mean for it to sound like I was criticizing her, but Paige took it that way.

"What was I supposed to do?"

"Nothing. I mean, that was great. I'm still trying to figure out how come you decided to sit way back here instead of walking right into Dad's waiting arms near the service station, that's all."

"Oh. Well, I knew he was there. He ran after me for a while but finally gave it up. I don't know why, but he wasn't able to run that fast. He called out that coyotes would eat my face off if I tried to spend a night in the woods, and then he headed back.

"I followed way behind, out of sight. I wanted to be sure of finding my way back, and I was pretty sure that Dad was my best chance. I got back about the time Dad pulled away in the car. But then I saw him cut through the woods from the highway. I didn't know what to do, so I sat down to wait and see what would happen.

"After a while, I got to thinking that you'd probably come look for me when I didn't show up, so I relaxed. When I heard you two coming, I said 'oops' to let you know I was here."

"What if it had been Dad coming?"

"Why would Dad come? He was sitting under a big old spruce tree waiting for us to come to him."

"See," I said to Cory, "I told you Paige was smart."

Paige gave me a whack in the dark.

"I couldn't be all that smart. Look at what I let you talk me into."

CHAPTER 7

THAT WAS THE COLDEST, HUNGRIEST NIGHT I'VE EVER spent. We huddled together off the trail in the dry gully and hoped that a bear wouldn't lumber by or coyotes come to eat our faces off. Along about daybreak, a familiar clank, clank, clank told us that Dad was driving away, and this time he was going a long way down the road.

Stiff as we were, we jumped up and hurried to the service station. If Dad had been smart enough to get someone to drive his car away for him, he'd have had us. But we didn't think about that, and, I guess, neither did he. There was nobody around the shabby old building except a man who was opening up and a friend of his who was lounging around drinking a big mug of coffee and smoking a cigarette. A sign said Open 6 A.M. to Midnight.

"Sure do," he was saying as we got close enough to hear. "Plan to ask her before the summer's out."

The old man laughed, and his face crinkled into a thousand wrinkles. "Why you old hoss thief. I know you. You'll never do it. Never in a million years."

"Sure I will. Why, Len, if you like, I'll give you a front row seat. I'll say, 'Abby, would you come over to Len's place please. There's somethin' important I want to ask you.' Let her figure that one out. You'll know the time has come when you see me bringing Abby in and settin' her down by the cash register."

They joked around some more, but I wasn't paying attention. I had noticed Len's friend's nearby pickup truck. It was nearly full of small, square bales of hay, and it had given me an idea.

"Look," Len said, clapping his friend on the back and walking into the garage with him, "all I want is an invitation to the wedding. The last thing I need is an invitation to the proposal!"

"Invitation to the wedding? Hell, I won't settle for less 'n you being my best man!"

"What? An old geezer like me!"

They disappeared from view. "Quick, into the back of the truck," I said.

"To where?" Paige asked.

"Who cares, as long as it's away from here?"

"I care." But she pulled herself over the tailgate anyway. I pushed Cory in after her and clambered in myself. A little rearranging, a little squeezing, and we were all hidden away amongst the hay. We lay there, warmer and more comfortable than we had been for a long time, and waited for Len's friend to decide it was time to hit the road.

About fifteen minutes later, he came out of the garage minus his coffee cup and lit a fresh cigarette.

"Well, now, don't work too hard."

They both laughed. It seemed strange to me. I mean, any man who ran a service station from six in the morning till midnight probably worked so hard it wasn't a laughing matter. Come to think of it, maybe he wasn't sixty years old at all. Maybe he was thirty-five and just worn out with work. I grinned to myself and then grinned even wider at the thought that I, Debbie Adaskin, was thinking up jokes at a time like this. Not bad for a basket case.

In fact, come to think of it, I hadn't been scratching since we'd made a break for it.

The slamming of the truck door broke into my thoughts. The driver started the engine, put the truck in gear and leaned out through the open window. "Gonna be a scorcher today."

"Amen," his friend replied, and we eased out of the service station and onto the highway.

We didn't have any idea where we were going, so of course we had no way of knowing if we were on the way home or heading even farther away.

An hour later, we reached a fair-sized town and slowed right down. I peeked at a banner over the road advertising rodeo days, and I gathered that the town we were pulling into was called Jackson. I didn't know if that was good news or bad.

Our driver pulled into a parking spot in front of a hardware store, and I pulled Cory and Paige out of the back of the truck.

"Why're we getting out?" Paige complained. "Maybe he's going farther."

"Yeah, and maybe he's going to unload the bales two blocks from here. We can't take that chance."

"Oh. Well, can we get something to eat then?"

I dug around in my blue jeans pocket and pulled out a handful of quarters.

"Ta-da! We eat."

"Hey, we're rich," Cory said.

"Let's find a restaurant fast, before I faint," Paige said.

"Uh-uh. No restaurants. This money has to last till

we get home. I'm going to buy us something cheap and filling at a grocery store, and you two are going to eat it without complaining. Got that?"

"Who died and made you boss," Paige grumbled.

"Aw, lighten up, Paige," Cory said. "It's her money. Let her buy what she wants."

So I bought cheese and a loaf of bread and a carton of orange juice, and we stuffed ourselves. It was the best-tasting food I ever remember eating, so I went back to the store to buy some more.

"Is that all we're ever going to eat—bread and cheese?" Paige asked.

"It's all they ever ate in *Heidi*," I said.

"In Heidi? Where's that?" she asked.

"Don't you remember that story about the little Swiss girl who was so lonely for her grandfather that she walked in her sleep? Well, that seemed to be all that they ever ate—goats' milk cheese and coarse, dry bread."

"And she still liked living with him?"

Cory laughed.

I was feeling so good I broke down and blew a few bucks on some granola bars and apples, and we jammed our pockets for later.

"And now we'd better get moving," I said. "Do I have as much hay sticking to me as you guys do?"

We looked one another over critically and decided we'd better do a clean-up job before our appearance attracted more attention than was good for us. We planned to use a service station washroom but ended up walking into a campground right in town, one of those awful places that packs people in elbow to elbow and bumper to bumper.

It was much better than a service station. For one

thing, we didn't have to ask for the key to the washroom. And, for another, it had showers.

We showered and dried off as well as we could with paper towels. Paige french braided my hair and said that I looked five years older that way.

Next, we found out where we were by snitching a map off a tourist bureau rack and finding Jackson on it.

Our ride had taken us farther from home.

"But that's okay," I reassured the kids. "Even if we picked all our rides just on how easy it was to hide in the back, chances are at least half of them would be heading the right way."

"How do you figure that?" Paige asked.

"Well, they can't all be going south, can they? Somebody has to be heading north."

"Ur, Debbie, I hate to tell you this," Paige said sarcastically, "but there are other directions, you know. There's east and west, too."

"Not here," I said, laughing. And it was true—Jackson is in a long valley between two mountain ranges, and the paved roads out of it head either north or south. Later, we might have to worry about being carried off to the east or west, but here we didn't. And here we were in a real tourist town with lots and lots of license plates from Canada. If only we dared ask someone for help!

But we didn't. So we started walking around town in search of a pickup truck heading north. Finally, we found one outside the Co-op—a truck with the Yellowstone forestry service logo on the side and a tarp stretched over the back with a few boxes and bags shoved in under it. We waited five anxious minutes for the coast to clear and then dived into the dark behind the boxes under the tarp.

That ride not only got us all the way back to Yellowstone, but it gave us a sheltered place to spend the night. But it was the end of the road for the truck. It wasn't going anywhere else, so we abandoned it in the morning and walked down the road a bit to a huge double parking lot. There were a lot of people off in the distance standing around, looking like they were waiting for something to happen, so I figured we had found ourselves the parking lot for Old Faithful. That's the geyser that spouts regularly just when people expect it to.

We went up and down the rows of vehicles looking for ones with Alberta license plates and especially for something we could hide in.

We tried a few doors on trailers and campers until one flew open in our faces and a huge, balding man came out yelling. He obviously thought we were trying to steal something, which, come to think of it, we were just about ready to do because there was no place we could see to buy any food and our granola bars and fruit were long gone.

"What the hell do you think you're doing?" the bald man shouted.

I immediately put my arms around Cory. The man saw that and thought, I guess, that Cory had been the one who turned his door knob. He shook his fist at us.

"You keep that kid under control, you hear? He'll get in trouble some day. Damned brat! I don't care how young he is. He's not poking his nose into my trailer. You hear?"

We backed away and the man slammed his door.

"'You hear?' I think the dead two states over must have heard," I said, laughing shakily.

Cory started to cry, and nobody could comfort him for a long time.

"C'mon, Cory," Paige finally said. "Like Mom always says—someday you'll laugh about this."

"No I won't. I want to go home."

"What I want to do even more than go home is eat," Paige said. "I think I'm about to start looking in garbage cans."

"They're bear-proof," I said sadly, "so I imagine they're Adaskin-proof, too."

"We could lower Cory by the ankles," Paige said hopefully.

Cory did such a shocked double take that we all burst out laughing.

Feeling a little better, we continued going up and down the parking lot. But now when we spotted a likely looking RV, we knocked on the door before we turned any knobs.

"Hey," I said when I saw a small trailer with a Disneyland sticker on it. "That one has to be going back to Alberta; it's already been to Disneyland." Paige knocked on the door while Cory and I hung back a few feet. We'd already agreed that if anybody answered the door, we'd come up and tell Paige she'd made a mistake, then get her out of there before anybody started yelling at her.

Nobody answered Paige's knock, so she knocked again, then turned the knob.

"Hey, it's open."

Quickly, I scanned the area around us. Nobody in sight.

"Is there any place inside to hide?"

"Not really. Maybe up on the bed. It's hard to see up there."

"Well, I guess we'd better get in."

"What if they come back and get in?" Paige asked.

"Then I'll try to look like I've had a bad bump on the head. You guys try to act surprised that strange people are walking into your trailer. In a little while we can all switch to acting confused that this isn't our trailer."

"It'll never work."

"Then just hope that they don't get in. Oh, and if they do, remember that we're traveling with our mom. Never, never let on that Dad's anywhere within five hundred miles."

I thought about that for a couple of minutes.

"Oh, and our name isn't Adaskin."

"Give it up," Paige groaned. "It won't work."

Cory ignored us both. He just went straight to the fridge and helped himself to some milk. I didn't have the heart to tell him he couldn't or to stop Paige either when she asked if she could have some. And after they'd each had a drink, it didn't seem to make a lot of difference if I had one, too.

A few minutes later, we heard the slamming of car doors very close to us, and the trailer lurched and began to roll forward. Soon it was rocking from side to side as we headed out of the parking lot and onto the road.

We didn't intend to help ourselves to anything more than milk, but we eventually broke down and stuffed ourselves on bananas and donuts, too, because the people who owned the trailer drove for hours before stopping.

CHAPTER 8

IT WASN'T LONG AFTER WE HIT THE ROAD THAT I FIGURED out we were going north and stopped worrying about our direction. That's when I started worrying about how we were going to get out of the trailer without being seen. Finally, I figured that our best bet was for me to jump out and run off alone, attracting all the attention to myself so Paige and Cory could get away without anyone noticing them. I hoped it wouldn't come to that—that we'd get a chance to sneak away—but I knew chances were against it.

Another thing I worried about at first was that we'd get just a few miles down the road before stopping. But, in fact, once the people in the car left Yellowstone, they seemed bent on getting as far as they could as fast as they could. They took only five minutes to fill up with gas and use the washroom—in the service station, thank God— and ten minutes to grab a hamburger at a drive-through. The rest of the time, they drove, and the place names we passed were all ones my map said we should be passing. I figured that apart from the problem of getting out of the trailer, we had it made.

After a few hours, things didn't look so good any-more. We were heading west along the road to St. Mary's and Glacier National Park instead of due north toward the border. I tried to get the kids ready to jump out if the trailer so much as stopped at a red light, but there just weren't any chances.

Once we pulled through the park gates into Glacier, I felt truly sick. We were driving into mountain wilderness, and I knew that meant cold nights and something worse.

"Paige, we've got to get out of here. This definitely doesn't look like a place with lots of grocery stores."

Paige looked out the window. "The sign says The Highway to the Sun. Wow!"

"The highway to starvation is more like it."

"There's plenty of food in here," Cory said.

"We've already snitched a carton of milk, a dozen donuts and six bananas. If we take any more, we're going to leave them without anything."

"So?" Paige said. "Have you got a better idea?"

I didn't. I poked around, and my mouth watered at a bag of nuts and raisins in one of the cupboards. There were bran muffins in another, and there was cheese in the fridge. If we'd been able to get off in the middle of farmland, I would have raided some farmer's garden and raspberry patch without minding a bit. Even hiding in the trailer and eating the food in the cupboards hadn't felt as criminal as actually planning to take food with us.

I looked out the window again at the dark green forest all around us and shrugged. The way I saw it, I didn't have much choice.

"Hey," Cory said suddenly. "You've got money left. We can pay them for the food."

We had less than five American dollars left, what with what we'd bought in Jackson and the exchange rate on our Canadian twenty. It was probably not enough to cover the price of the nuts, the muffins and the cheese, let alone the stuff we'd already gobbled up, but it made us feel very rich and virtuous, so we took a small package of sliced ham, too.

We turned in at a view point overlooking a lake with an island in the middle, and our people got out of their car to take a look. I was absolutely shaking with excitement and delight at being able to make such an easy getaway.

But as soon as I tried to open the door, I found we couldn't get away at all. The trailer was too close to one of those bear-proof garbage containers. Not even Paige was skinny enough to squeeze through the crack.

So we sat there for the longest five minutes of my life—the trailer absolutely still, nobody watching the door, our pockets full of food and still not able to slip away. What hurt worst of all was knowing we'd be going farther and farther from home just as soon as the trailer pulled back onto that blasted Highway to the Sun.

The next time we stopped, we were high up in the Logan Pass at an interpretive center with a huge parking lot. The driver got out his door, and I had a sudden inspiration. I started tapping with a spoon on a vent on the driver's side of the trailer. He stopped and listened, shushed his wife, who was getting out of her door, and walked back along the side of the trailer to where I was making the noise. His wife came around to that side, too.

"Fast."

It was all I had to say. Paige and Cory slipped out the door and disappeared down the rows of parked cars and RVs. As soon as I was sure they were gone, I stopped tapping and ran for the door myself.

The trailer rocked as I jumped out, but I was dodging

and ducking faster than I can usually run straight out. I knew I must have covered a lot of distance before either of them figured out what was happening or recovered from their surprise and ran around to the trailer door.

It was easy to mingle unnoticed in the crowds, and I was sure the trailer people hadn't caught so much as a glimpse of us. Still, I kept my eye out for signs of them or anybody obviously searching for somebody, and I breathed a deep sigh of relief when I saw them pulling back out onto the highway.

Paige and Cory and I got back together at the large wooden map showing the hiking trails in the park.

"Look," I said, pointing, "there's a trail going straight from here up to Waterton Lake."

"So?"

"So that's in Canada. It's due north of here and not very far."

"What's 'due north'?" Cory asked.

"It means straight north."

I put my thumb on one side of the scale and my baby finger on the other. Then I walked the gap between them up the Great Wall trail.

"According to the scale, it's about twenty miles."

"How much is twenty miles?" Paige asked.

"About thirty kilometers. I heard people usually walk about five kilometers an hour. That means we can do it in a day. That's better than trying to walk back along the highway and getting picked up by the police before we've gone two kilometers. Or catching another ride and ending up at the coast . . . or back at Yellowstone."

Paige squinted off across the high alpine meadow with its millions of yellow flowers. A rocky trail wound across it and actually looked kind of inviting.

"I suppose it's a lot farther by road," she said.

I pulled out my map and showed her just how much farther it was.

"But aren't there bears?" Cory asked.

"There's lots of hikers," I said. "I don't think there'd be bears on the hiking trails."

"If there're lots of hikers, won't they have a cow when they see us?"

"No," I said, "because I'm a lot older than I look. And you two are my children."

"They'll still think it's funny that we don't have a backpack."

"It'll be over the next hill where we ditched it while we went exploring."

"God, you're getting to be a good liar," Paige said. She looked again at the map. "It looks so easy on the map. . . ."

"It'll be dark soon," I said, not giving her time to change her mind. "We should get going now."

"It's getting downright cold," Paige said, shivering. "Couldn't we spend the night in the interpretive center?"

We looked the center over, but we couldn't find a good hiding place. We gave it up when we found something almost as good tied up in bundles by the back door—several armfuls of clean newspapers. With those, I knew we'd be able to keep warm in a sheltered spot out on the trail.

Paige wasn't so sure. "Newspapers! You've got to be kidding."

"Lighten up. I've seen guys sleeping in the park with just a paper or two on top of them. Mom says they're great for insulation. That's why she put big piles of them up in the attic—to shut out the drafts and keep more heat in the house. Remember?"

Paige still looked doubtful, but she took an armful of papers anyway. We shoved some inside our shirts, front and back, and rolled the rest as well as we could so people would have to look closely to see what we were carrying.

After a good wash, we stuffed our pockets with toilet paper and headed out onto the Great Wall trail. We walked casually and slowly—obviously three kids whose folks had said they could go for a walk as long as they didn't go far—and soon the interpretive center was a little box far behind us on the horizon.

Night didn't come to the mountaintop till long after the valleys had filled up with shadows. We walked quickly once we were away from the center, glad to be moving again after the long day cooped up in the trailer.

When it did get quite dark, we made ourselves a little nest out of the wind in a small dip behind some boulders. The ground was springy soft with a carpet of some kind of plant, the newspapers were fairly windproof and warm, and the sky was ablaze with millions of stars.

"Wow," Cory said, "it's beautiful!"

"There's Orion," Paige said. "Look, Cory. Those are the stars in his sword. . . . That's his belt . . . and his shoulders."

Orion, the hunter.

I wondered what Dad was doing. I wondered if he was worried sick about us.

I remembered being a little kid riding on his back while he tore around the house. I had been scared stiff at being up so high, and I had hung on tight to his hair and squealed with excitement. Paige had been a baby in a small wooden cradle then, so that must have been when I was three.

Those were the days when Dad called me Flower and

had me root around in his jacket pocket for the pieces of fudge he bought me on his way home. And those were the days when he used to sing work songs like "Old Man River" and "Sixteen Tons" in a deep voice that vibrated through my whole body as I lay on his chest.

The stars blurred as I remembered. But they cleared again as I remembered more—Christmases when we got games advertised in TV commercials that showed families laughing and playing together, but that we didn't play together because Mom and Dad were fighting over how the tree should have been decorated; times when Dad promised he'd have us a game of baseball, but he never showed up even though we waited for him till dark; times when his idea of fun was teasing us about the words we couldn't say right, the things we couldn't do. He had a routine that involved Cory drooling and sticking a fork in his eye, but it never struck me as funny because it always made Cory feel stupid.

"I'm glad I'm here," Paige said suddenly. "I can't believe it."

"What can't you believe? That you're here? Or that you're glad?"

"Both. I'll bet that lots of people live to be a hundred without ever sleeping under the stars on top of a mountain. But to be doing it alone. I always thought it was a horribly scary thing to be alone."

"Well, it is."

"Not nearly as scary as being around other people," Paige said positively. "Up here, I don't expect to meet a mass murderer. In fact, I'd be very surprised if I did."

Cory laughed wickedly and went into something like a Freddie Kruger routine, I guessed. "Surprise!" he said. "There's one mass murderer up here."

Cory's usually so quiet. He took us completely by surprise, and we laughed till our stomachs ached.

"The worst is over now," I said. "For one thing, we'll be in Canada soon. In fact, maybe we already are; it's hard to tell."

"How long till Mom gets back home?" Cory asked

I counted on my fingers. It had taken us two days to get to Vancouver. We'd stayed there a full day, and then we'd run away on the fourth day after that. In all, we'd been away nine days. Allow a day to walk to Waterton, and we'd have four days to get home before Mom started wondering where we were.

"Five days," I said.

"Five days isn't so awfully long. We can wait for Mom at home, no problem," Paige said. "I hope Dad isn't still searching for us in the woods back of that garage."

"Naw," I said. "He knows we ran away. He's got to figure we're heading home. Why would he hang around there?"

"Well, I hope he doesn't think a mass murderer got us," Cory said.

"No way," I assured him. But I wondered.

The next morning, we ate ham slices and a bran muffin each and started to walk. The sun was warm from the moment it rose. Later on, it got downright hot. The air was clear and sweet. Sometimes we sat down, not because we were tired, but just because we loved to look at the wild flowers, the alpine meadows stretching away at our feet and the ramparts of the mountains towering above the meadows.

We did see a bear—a very big brown bear—off down the hillside below us. It was a long way away but not so far that you couldn't see how scruffy and balding its coat looked in patches or how small its eyes were. The bear stood up on its hind legs and snuffed the air as we tiptoed by on the path above, but then it dropped to all fours and started scratching behind one ear just like a dog with fleas.

"See. They don't come up on the hiking trails," I said with all the confidence I could muster, but my legs felt wobbly and my hands were shaking.

Paige gave me a funny look, but she didn't say anything.

There weren't a lot of hikers. We talked to the second batch we met late in the evening, when we figured we must be just a mile or two from Waterton.

"Hi," they said. "Your folks couldn't keep up with you?"

"I guess it's the heavy packs," I said. "How much farther to Waterton?"

They stopped and shifted their top-heavy loads. There'd been a lot of uphill and downhill lately, and they were both sweating a lot.

"Well . . . let's see. We figure we must be just about halfway to the Logan Pass. That'd make it about fifteen miles."

"Fifteen miles?" Paige turned accusing eyes on me.

"Dad'll be glad to hear that," I said and gave Cory a little push in the small of his back. He sighed and started moving again.

Paige was sputtering mad. "You dork. You said it was about twenty miles."

"Sorry."

"I'm tired," Cory said.

He didn't need to tell me. We'd been dragging a bit since noon and a lot since late afternoon. Our feet were hurting, too.

"Fifteen miles," Paige said.

"So? What's your point?"

She looked like she was about to start beating on me, so I took a hasty step backward and apologized for real.

"I am sorry, Paige," I said. "I didn't know. But even if I had known, I still think we had to come this way. Let's stop now and fix everything up so we'll be really comfortable and we'll feel okay tomorrow. It's not so bad. It's another night under the stars."

"I'm glad we're getting to stay on this trail two days," Cory said. "This is almost like a real holiday."

Paige looked worried. "I just wish we'd saved more of our food."

"We've got enough food," I said. "The funny thing is that the more you walk, the less hungry you get. Now let's find ourselves a good spot."

We found one by a little stream, and it felt very good on our sore feet. We made our nest even snugger than the night before, but I had to admit I didn't feel exactly great knowing we were fifteen miles either way from civilization. One thing that made me feel better was knowing that, at half way, we were probably sleeping right on the border between Canada and the States. I'd never slept on an international border before.

CHAPTER 9

WHEN I WOKE UP THE NEXT MORNING, I DIDN'T KNOW AT first where I was. The warm sun on my face made me think I was home in bed, where sometimes the sun hit my face in just that way. I expected to hear Mom moving around downstairs and to smell toast and coffee, maybe even frying bacon.

The sound of crinkling newspaper and the fresh mountain air reminded me that Mom was a long way away, so I snuggled down sleepily, too lazy to mind very much.

Mom isn't perfect. Lord knows, if you were going to rate her impatience on a scale of one to ten, she'd be an eleven-and-a-half. But that's mainly when she's worried about something. She used to be worried all the time when she was married to Dad, but since they got divorced, she's gotten younger and funnier. She's even gotten prettier. Anyway, even if Mom isn't perfect, us kids are first in her life. It's a very safe feeling, knowing that.

Paige yawned and stretched beside me. A bird trilled as though its heart would burst with joy. I opened my eyes and looked up at the patterns a stunted little pine tree made against the vivid blue of the sky. At that moment, I felt as though I would never be afraid again.

It struck me that I'd been scared a lot. In fact, I'd been

scared most of my life. I hated that feeling. It was like slogging through knee-deep mud, lugging a heavy pack on my back. It was like riding in an elevator that was always lurching downward unexpectedly. Or trying to walk a narrow ledge high above jagged rocks. Or inching down dark, rickety stairs into a strange, pitch-black basement.

But where would I be without my fear? Doesn't fear keep a person safe?

Lord knows, the world is full of frightening things.

But that day, way back in the high country, the world didn't seem so bad. It was full of sunshine and wild flowers; turquoise lakes and soft-eyed, shy deer; fleecy clouds sweeping over sharp, gray peaks; and waterfalls like bridal veils. Though we were tired and getting hungry, we almost didn't want to reach Waterton.

Until, that is, we came over a ridge and were hit full blast by an icy wind. Then we shoved newspapers into every part of our clothes that would hold them, and we quickened our steps. Suddenly, we couldn't wait to get to Waterton.

Waterton refused to come into view. The day got colder. The wind began to sting. It was driving a combination of rain and sleet that soaked through our clothes and newspapers and turned our fingers blue. Desperate to get to shelter, we raced along, slipping on the slick trail and falling again and again. Water streamed down our faces and steam rose off our backs. We were blinded and our feet were numb.

For the first time since we'd made a break for it, I seriously considered the possibility that we might die. Even after the squall passed and the rain stopped, we were in serious trouble. Cory was staggering. I didn't know at the time that it was a sign of hypothermia, but I knew it had to be bad news.

We were too tired to go on, but we didn't dare stop. In fact, we were so intent on continuing that we almost went right by the campground without even seeing it. But finally we did see it, and, better yet, we spotted the ladies washroom. We hauled Cory in there and shoved him into a shower stall. Even before we got him out of his clothes, we turned the water on hot and kept turning him like a little chicken on a barbecue.

Then we got ourselves stalls and thawed out. The miracle is that they had enough hot water to do the job. Eventually, we stopped shivering and started thinking about getting out of the shower.

"What do we do now?" Paige called out.

"I don't know. . . . Wring out our clothes and put them back on I guess."

"Yuck."

I thought for a while. "Give me just your T-shirts. I'll dry them under the thing that blows hot air on your hands."

"And what if someone comes in and sees you without any clothes on?"

"Paige, don't be an idiot! I'll have my clothes on."

I wished, though, that I had taken a chance on nobody coming in because nobody did. At first, I thought maybe it was because it was too cold for the people with RV plumbing to bother to go outside to a washroom. Later, when I went out to build a fire for drying our jeans, I realized that it was probably because there was hardly anybody in the campground at all.

Someone had left a fire burning in the picnic shelter, however. I built it up to a crackling blaze and toasted myself and an armful of clothes in front of it. Later, the kids came out of the washroom in just their T-shirts and toasted themselves around it, too.

We even dried newspapers and restuffed ourselves. It took several hours, and by the time we were done, we were ready to keel over with hunger.

I had kind of hoped that someone would come to cook in the picnic shelter and would offer us something to eat, but it seemed that no one was using either the washroom or the picnic shelter that stabbingly cold night. I looked longingly at the two or three RVs in the campground, and I ached to be behind one of those snug, bright little windows.

"Stay here and keep the fire up," I ordered Paige and Cory. "I'm going to look around, see if I can find anything to eat."

I circled the campground, stopping on the far edge under some trees where a van sat with an awning pulled over a picnic table. A lone figure sat hunched over a small campfire. I walked a little closer, drawn against my will by the wonderful aroma of stew. Meat and carrots and onions and lots of pepper. My mouth watered till I positively drooled.

The figure by the fire unfolded itself and gave the pot a stir. It turned out to be an old man with wispy white hair and light blue eyes. He was crying.

Ordinarily, I find the sight of adults crying about the scariest thing there is. But in the situation we were in, it was kind of reassuring. . . . I guess it gave me hope that this was someone who could understand how we felt.

I cleared my throat and waited. The old man looked up, wiped his nose on his sleeve and squinted in my general direction. He looked scared enough for two.

"Who's there?"

"Excuse me," I said. "I didn't mean to startle you."

"Why, it's a child! What do you want?"

"Uh, I wondered if I could . . . chop some wood for you in exchange for some of whatever it is that's in that pot. It sure smells good!"

"Oh, it does, does it?" the old man said sharply. "Step out into the light where I can see you. . . . That's better. Why, you're a girl!"

"Yes," I said self-consciously, "I am."

"You're hungry?"

"Yes," I said more definitely. "I sure am."

"How come?"

"Uh . . . it's a long story."

That "it's a long story" is usually a pretty good line. I know it's shut me up lots of times. But not this little old man.

"You're a runaway, aren't you?"

"No," I said. "I'm trying to get home."

"Why don't you go to the police?"

"It's a long story," I said again but this time with less confidence.

"Indeed." He looked me up and down. "You must be freezing . . . out in weather like this, dressed like that."

"I am cold. It was nice until just a few hours ago."

"Where did you come from? It snowed here this morning."

"I came off one of the trails from Glacier National Park," I said. "I really am awfully hungry, so if you want me to chop wood before you feed me, you'll have to let me do it now because I don't think I could answer all your questions and then do it."

He jumped up and fetched a jacket out of the van. "Here, put this on, and sit down and have some stew."

I put on the jacket and took the bowl of stew he ladled out for me. "I'll be right back."

"What do you mean you'll be right back? Where are you going?"

"Nowhere. I'll leave your jacket here if that's what you're worried about."

He peered over my shoulder in the general direction of the picnic shelter. "There's someone with you, isn't there?"

I sighed. "Yes."

"Your boyfriend?"

"No. My brother and sister."

"And they're hungry, too."

It didn't really seem to require an answer.

"Oh, very well," he sighed. "Bring them over. There's enough for all of us."

I put down the stew and was off in a flash. The old man looked horrified when he saw Paige and Cory. "Good God," he muttered and began rooting around in his van. He handed each of the kids a sweater, then rooted around some more and pulled out an old blanket for them to wrap up in. They sat down by the fire, and let him bundle them up and put bowls of stew in their hands. I saw tears in Paige's eyes, and I turned away because I hadn't come through so much without crying only to start now.

In a minute, we were all slurping down delicious hot stew and stuffing bread in our mouths. The old man watched us eat without saying anything, only taking some stew for himself when we'd had refills and couldn't have managed another mouthful.

"The campground sure is empty," I said, hoping to start a conversation that wouldn't turn sticky right away.

"It was packed last night," the man said. "But when the weather turned cold and the forecast was for more of the same, they all packed up and moved on."

"How come you didn't?" Paige asked.

"I thought about it," he said, "but the timing's all wrong. You see, I have reservations at the William Watson Lodge for the day after tomorrow. Not long enough to go somewhere else, though a little long for sitting around here in bad weather. I don't know. Maybe I should head up to the Kananaskis now, even if they're having rain there, too."

We weren't sure what he was talking about, so we didn't say anything. He smiled. "I can hardly wait to get indoors and put my feet up in front of a fireplace for a week. The long-range forecast isn't good."

"Are you going into an old folks home?" Cory asked.

"Good gracious, no. What would make you ask me that?"

I knew it had to do with our great-grandfather staying in a place called Sunset Lodge before he died, but I didn't like to explain about that.

But the man figured Cory out for himself. "Oh," he said, "I'll bet you've never heard of William Watson Lodge. It's a beautiful place in the mountains that disabled people and senior citizens can stay in for four dollars a night. It wasn't easy to get reservations there at this time of year. You see, the disabled have first crack at available space. Us seniors get whatever's left over."

"Oh," Cory said politely.

"Too bad about the weather," Paige said.

"So," the old man said, setting down his bowl and turning to me, "now I think you have a long story to tell me."

"Shouldn't I chop your wood first?"

"No hurry," he said and waited.

I didn't know how to begin. The old people I've known want to do all the talking, or they want to listen so they can laugh about how cute I am or point out to me how wrong I am. I've pretty much learned to keep my mouth shut around old people.

But since I had to say something, it was maybe a good idea to figure this man out so I could say the right thing. I mean, if he wanted cute, I'd give him cute.

"Dad kidnapped us," Cory blurted out.

The man stared at Cory for a minute and then looked at me. "Did he?"

There went cute. "Yes," I said.

"Your parents are divorced?"

"Yes."

"Why didn't you go to the police?"

"The police came to us, but it turned out that Dad had papers. I know there had to be something wrong with them, but they looked right to the police."

"Forgeries. Easy as pie. Court documents are fill-in-the-blanks, and you don't even have to have a matching typewriter."

"For a minute or two there, even I believed he had custody. Then he pulled out a letter I'd started to write complaining about having to travel with him, and he convinced everybody it meant I didn't like him having custody. After that . . . well, I knew when I was licked."

He laughed and I found myself laughing, too.

"Of course, it wasn't funny," he said.

"No."

"Well," he said, "that wasn't so long a story after all. Did you run away from him in Glacier National Park?"

"No. Down south of Yellowstone."

He shook his head. "You're lucky. I hate to think of what could have happened between there and here."

He stared thoughtfully into the fire for a bit.

"Where's home?" he asked suddenly.

"A little southeast of Edmonton. At least for the next two weeks."

"Oh, really? I'm from Edmonton, too," he said. "We had the loveliest little house near the university. It had a stained-glass window and french doors on the study so that the fire in the fireplace there brightened the whole downstairs, and it had a conservatory, too. That's a sort of indoor greenhouse," he added, seeing, I suppose, that we didn't understand.

"I used to grow herbs and tomatoes and lettuce for salads all year round. That irritated my wife unbearably because she believed that conservatories should be for flowers." He laughed. "Oh, well. It was a lovely little house." He blinked fast and cleared his throat.

"I'll drive you home tomorrow. That'll just beautifully fill the time between now and checking into the lodge."

"But that's a long way to drive," I said, "just to drive someone home."

"If someone can go home," he said, "it's worth going halfway around the world. You're lucky you have a home." He nodded toward the van. "This is my home for the time being."

Then he took a big white handkerchief out of his back pocket and blew his nose long and loud.

CHAPTER 10

WE LOOKED AT ONE ANOTHER AND AT THE OLD MAN, AND then I jumped up and started chopping wood.

By the time I had a neat little pile of firewood, the man had done the dishes and the kids were half asleep, propped up against each other.

"Good work," he said, nodding toward my little pile of wood.

It struck me that he was quite capable of cutting his own wood, but he had probably let me do it so I wouldn't feel like a horrible mooch.

"Are you feeling better?" I asked.

"Oh, don't worry about me," he said. "Sometimes I get to feeling sorry for myself. But then I think of how very lucky I really am, and I'm fine again."

"Is the van really the only home you've got now?"

"Yup." It came out more a gulp than a word.

"What happened to your house?" Actually, I wasn't sure I wanted answers to any of my questions, but it seemed rude not to ask.

"Let's put the children to bed," he said, "and then I'll tell you."

That kind of knocked me over. For one thing, though I often thought of Paige and Cory as "the kids," it felt good having an adult do the same thing without including me. For another thing, he'd said, "Let's put the children to bed." If we were really going to do that . . . well, it was a big load off my mind.

"Where?"

"Why, in the van, of course. There's plenty of room. I can clear a space on the floor, and it'll be more comfortable than sleeping on the ground at any rate. Also, I packed too much bedding. I'll use the sleeping bag and give you the comforter and a few blankets. . . . You'll be just fine. Why don't you take your brother and sister to the washroom? I'll have everything ready when you get back."

"I can't believe how cold it is," I said when we got back. And it was. In fact, snowflakes were falling gently around us, lightly sugaring the ground.

"Waterton's like that," he said. "It can snow here any month of the year . . . and usually does. I should have gone to Banff."

"I'm glad you didn't."

Paige and Cory climbed into the van and burrowed under the comforter with their clothes on. Even before I finished tucking them in, they zonked right out. I pulled the van door shut and went back to the fire the old man had built up.

"Here," he said. "I made you some hot chocolate."

I thanked him and sat down on a log end with a sigh of contentment.

"By the way, I never thought to ask you your names. Mine is Dusty. Dustin Andover."

"I'm Debby," I said. "My sister's Paige and my brother's Cory. Are you related to Dustin Hoffman?" I guess that's about the stupidest thing I've ever said, but I was tired and not thinking very clearly. Dustin Andover took it as a very clever joke, however, and laughed more than it deserved even if it had been a joke.

"What happened to your house?"

"I spent it."

"You spent it?"

"I'm sorry," he said. "I suppose I'm talking in riddles. What I should have said is that I sold the house and spent all the money I got from it—that and a lot more money besides."

He chuckled. "If you ever want to irritate your children, just spend their inheritance right out from under their noses. That'll do it."

"Well, it was your money. What did you spend it on? Of course," I added hastily, "you don't have to tell me. It's none of my business."

He stared into the fire so long that I thought he wasn't going to tell me. But then he spoke softly, as though to himself. "She was worth it. Every penny."

This didn't sound like stuff an old man should be telling a young girl. I took a long swallow of hot chocolate and tried to think of something else to talk about.

"Of course, mind you, the children thought she was worth it, too. They just didn't think I knew what I was doing . . . that it would do any good."

After another long pause, he turned and looked piercingly at me. "If your mother was dying of cancer, would you run all over North America trying out every quack cure that somebody advertised as the newest breakthrough in cancer research?"

"Your wife was dying of cancer?"

"Did die. None of it did any good. Two hundred and fifty thousand dollars, you see, and I couldn't save her. In the end, it turned out that the kids were right."

"I'm so sorry."

He turned his head away, and his voice was muffled for a moment. "Well, yeah, you know how it is. These things happen."

"And that's why you're living in a van?" I asked, unable to believe that such a thing could be true.

"Next thing to a bag lady," he said with an unexpected chuckle. "But it's temporary. I hope it's temporary. I'm living off just my pension till we fight it all out in court."

"Your kids and you?"

"Yup. They want me declared mentally incompetent. They think they should put the little bit of money I have left in a trust fund and administer it for me. You know, put me on an allowance. Now I ask you, now that Rose is dead, am I likely to run off and blow the rest?"

"It's your money. So what if you did?"

"I never thought I'd be fighting them like this. Who cares about money if Rose is gone? But now those kids've gone and got me mad, and I'm going to fight back. It's not the money; it's having my children put in charge of me. That's what I can't stand. Even if I starve, I won't stand for it."

He looked too weak to put up much of a fight. On second thought, the way his eyes flashed when he said he'd rather starve, maybe there was more to him than I'd thought at first.

"Anyway, that's why I'm living in this van. By sticking to campgrounds where seniors can stay free or for half price, I've managed to cut my living expenses down to practically nothing." He smiled a slow, happy smile. "And, you know, though I get low sometimes, really it's been fun. It gives me such a feeling of satisfaction to know they couldn't control me like they thought they could.

"Who would ever believe an old man like me would just up and hit the road rather than knuckle under? Who would ever believe that an old man like me could tough it out? But I've been doing this for six weeks, and I know I can manage at least till September and the start of the cold weather."

We looked around us at the fine dusting of snow on everything, and we both broke out laughing.

"Anyway," he went on, "I've been thinking it would be fun to go down to Arizona . . . to live in the van for the winter in a nice warm place." He turned to me. "There are campgrounds around Phoenix where just about everybody is retired, and they play bridge and square dance all the time. You know, I think I could hold out against those kids even if I lost my case in court."

I looked at Dustin Andover, who struck his family as downright stupid and looked as fragile as dandelion fluff, and I felt a strong urge to hug him. Sitting there with snowflakes melting on my nose in the middle of July, talking about awful things like quarreling and dying, I felt a big bubble of happiness expanding inside, and I didn't have the foggiest notion why I felt so good.

"Have you talked to your children lately?" I asked.

"Nope. No reason to that I can think of."

"That's kind of sad . . . not talking to your own kids."

"Yes, it is. But, as you know, that's the way it is sometimes."

I was surprised to find myself feeling a twinge of sympathy for Dad. I tried to squelch it, but it wouldn't stay squelched. He'd done some pretty dumb things, but in his eyes, it had all been somehow noble. Maybe like spending a fortune trying to save the life of someone you loved.

"I'm beat," I said, putting an end to the conversation with Mr. Andover and my own uncomfortable thoughts.

The next morning, there was a few centimeters of snow on the ground, so we hit the road without breakfast and only stopped to make pancakes when we got out onto the prairie, where it was warmer and there was no snow. Paige had a cold. Not only did her nose run constantly, but she was starting to cough a harsh little bark of a cough that sounded like it must be cutting her up inside. She spent the long drive up through Calgary and Red Deer curled up in a ball under Mr. Andover's comforter. I held Cory on my lap and sat in the passenger seat just staring out the window.

After struggling so hard and worrying so much, I let my mind go blank as I gazed at the vast, rolling prairie and left everything up to the white-haired old man who sat tooling that van down the highway at over a hundred kilometers an hour.

From time to time, something he saw would stir him up to tell stories about his childhood on a Saskatchewan farm, where his little room up under the eaves had been boiling hot in the summer and freezing cold in winter, where the dust was already blowing before the mud in the yard had dried or the snow against the north side of the barn had melted, where you carried your shoes to school and then put them on because nobody could afford to keep buying kids new shoes all the time.

I didn't say much. I didn't even hear half of what he said, but he didn't seem to mind. He just kept on about how cows liked warm hands and would kick you if your hands were cold and about how you could skate for miles on country sloughs. . . . Stuff like that.

More and more, what he said was punctuated with little spurts of coughing from the back.

We took a break for sandwiches not far from Red Deer, got the tank filled with gas and headed out on the last leg of the drive home. Mr. Andover was looking awfully tired, but he insisted he was okay.

"In fact," he said, "I'm better than okay. I'm going to go into Edmonton after I drop you off and see an old friend of mine. After a nice visit, I'll be right as rain and ready to head out tomorrow to Kananaskis country. Maybe I'll even be able to talk my friend into joining me at William Watson Lodge for a week. I wish I had thought of it sooner. I hope he'll come."

With plans like that, Mr. Andover almost made me feel as though we'd done him a favor, dragging him hundreds of kilometers out of his way to get us safely home. And with plans like that, he was in a hurry. He took us right up to the house but didn't stick around.

"I see your mom's not here," he said. "Is there a neighbor you can go to till she gets home?"

"Sure," I said. "We can go to the Wallenbergs down the road."

"Good," he said. "Well, take care. Better give Paige some cough syrup and keep her in bed. Good luck."

"Thank-you for everything," I said. "Sure hope everything goes okay for you."

"Oh," he smiled. "It will. Same as for you."

I watched him drive away. I watched the driveway long after he had disappeared behind the trees. That's when I remembered that Jason's family was at the lake.

"Well," I said kind of sadly, "I guess we're on our own again."

"At leeds we're home," Paige said snuffling. "Oh, Debbie, I am so cauwd."

Her face looked hot, but she was shivering.

"C'mon," I said, feeling around under the porch for the front door key, "let's get you inside and into a hot bathtub."

"Can I go over to Jason's house?" Cory asked.

"How cad you?" Paige asked. "Arendt they at the lake?"

That didn't strike me as much of a problem just then or even for an hour or two afterward. Mom might not be home for two days. So what? Big deal. We could take care of ourselves for a couple of days. There was plenty of food in the house, and everything was working. I mean, nobody had turned off the water or the electricity or anything. This would be a piece of cake.

But Paige got worse and worse. I poured cough syrup into her and gave her Tylenol and rubbed Vicks on her chest, but nothing seemed to help. Her skin felt fiery to the touch, and her eyes looked kind of unfocused and funny.

I was beginning to feel a new kind of fear.

It began to rain, so Cory settled himself down in front of the TV with his quilt wrapped around him. He was quite happy to be making up for lost time with an overdose of TV, and I was quite happy to have one less kid to worry about.

I made up a can of frozen orange juice and held a glassful up to Paige's chattering teeth. She sipped at it but threw it all up five minutes later. I gave her just plain water, but she threw that up, too.

"I want M-Mom," she cried as I wiped up her mess. "Oh, Debbie, I hurd so mudch."

"Shh. It'll be okay," I said. "I'm doing all the things that Mom does when we get sick like this." I smoothed her hair away from her face. "Would you like to watch TV? I mean, would it take your mind off things?"

Paige looked at me as though she didn't hear me or understand what I was saying. Her cheeks were wet with tears, but she didn't seem to notice. Then suddenly she shuddered and began hugging herself more tightly.

"I'm so cauwd. Can'd you warm me up?"

"Oh, Paige, I've got you smothered in blankets. Just hang on. You'll be feeling better soon. I've got to go downstairs now and get something for Cory to eat."

And me.

I was hungry, too, but I felt it would have been mean to mention it when Paige was suffering so much.

"Don'd leave me," she squeaked, grabbing my arm.

"I've got to. But just for a minute."

Her eyes were wide and dark with fear. This was not my Paige. She looked a little bit crazy.

"Hey, take it easy. Cory will sit with you," I promised.

I pulled Cory away from his precious TV and went into the kitchen to make up a package of macaroni and cheese. Later, we ate up in the bedroom to keep Paige company.

Not that it did much good. She huddled under the covers and didn't even seem to notice we were there.

Finally, she fell asleep, but it was an uneasy, twitching sleep. Her eyes kept rolling, and her lips kept moving. Still, it was a relief for me, and I hoped for her, to have her semi-unconscious for a while.

I went downstairs and did up the dishes and stared out the window at the gray, dripping trees and the little rivulets of water running through our backyard. The gloom of that dark, soggy scene pulled me down.

When I saw that Cory had fallen asleep in front of the TV, I pulled his quilt up around his ears, shut off the TV and just sat there staring at the carpet, torturing myself with all the times I'd told on Paige and had gotten her into trouble. Sometimes I'd accused her of things she hadn't even done, and Mom had believed me.

I shut off the light and went upstairs to watch Paige toss and turn. Maybe I should be calling a doctor. Maybe I should be wrapping her up in cold, wet sheets. Maybe she would die, and it would all be my fault.

The rain had stopped drumming on the roof, and, except for Paige's rough breathing, the house was quiet. I realized it was late—close to midnight—and I should be getting to bed or I'd be too wiped to do anything the next day.

Clank, clank, clank.

I sat there listening to the distant noise that was coming closer. At first, I was so numb that it didn't make much of an impression on me.

Clank, clank, clank.

Suddenly, I stiffened and my hand shot out all by itself and turned out the little bedside lamp.

Dad!

CHAPTER 11

THE CLANKING OF DAD'S OLD CAR STOPPED. I STOOD UP, but I was rooted to the spot. I simply couldn't think what to do. Then it occurred to me that Dad couldn't possibly think we were home. The first thing I had to do, then, was get to Cory and make sure he didn't wake up and give us all away.

I groped my way to the top of the stairs and stopped to listen. Silence—the kind you get in horror movies just before something awful jumps out of the shadows. I made my way as quietly down the creaky stairs as I could manage and listened again. More silence.

I had forgotten for the moment that all the curtains had been washed and packed in boxes late in June. It had been an easy way for Mom to get the jump on packing because nobody really needs curtains when your nearest neighbor is half a mile away. From the shadows at the bottom of the stairs, I viewed the bare windows with alarm.

Any minute, Dad might be stepping onto the porch. Any minute now, he might be knocking at the door loud enough to wake up Cory. I darted out of the shadows and over to the couch. As I knelt down, I put a hand over Cory's mouth.

"Shh, Cory, don't make a sound."

He woke up and instinctively began struggling.

"Cory, it's me—Debbie," I hissed. "Lie still and listen to me. I just heard Dad driving up. Do you understand? We have to be quiet so he won't know we're here."

Cory nodded his head, and I took my hand away from his mouth. I could see the whites of his eyes even in the dark of such a cloudy night.

"What're we going to do?" he whispered.

"Hold tight and keep quiet," I answered.

We waited for a knock at the door.

"Can he get in?" Cory asked.

I hadn't thought of that. Would Dad try to get in? Could he? Of course he could! Not with a key because we'd taken the one that was usually kept under the porch for emergencies. But a man like Dad surely didn't need a key. He was fully capable of breaking a window if it came to that.

But it wouldn't have to come to that. We'd opened a window to get some fresh air because the house was stale from being shut up for ten days. If Dad saw that open window . . .

Let's face it. He didn't need an open window any more than he needed a key, but the window was a dead giveaway that we were home. Mom would never leave a downstairs window open while she went away for two weeks. And Dad wasn't likely to believe Mom had come back early with no car outside the house or tire tracks along the muddy driveway.

But wait! There would be tire tracks on the driveway. There'd be Mr. Andover's tire tracks. If Dad saw them, he'd think Mom might have come back early, though he wouldn't be sure as long as he didn't see her car parked outside the house. I wished I knew if Dad had come looking for us or if he'd come to tell Mom that we were missing.

Whichever it was, he was probably majorly interested in knowing if we'd made it home. In fact, it'd be really important to him to know who was giving the house its lived-in look—Mom or us. Till he knew that, he probably wouldn't actually do anything. That was a comforting thought.

I needed a comforting thought about then because I looked up at the window nearest me and saw Dad's face pressed to the glass, his head framed by his hands as he peered inside.

I scrunched down so I wasn't anything but a lump on the floor—a darker shadow among dark shadows. Cory, lying on the couch, was out of sight of the window, but I was in full view with only darkness to hide me. I hoped that my moving hadn't caught Dad's eye.

Maybe it had. Dad didn't move from the window for a long time. When he did move, it was only to peer in the next window and the one after that.

I didn't have to tell Cory what was up. As soon as I ducked, I felt him pulling the quilt over his head. Neither of us moved a muscle until I was sure that Dad had gone on to the kitchen windows.

"Quick. Upstairs."

Cory jumped up and ran for the stairs, dragging his quilt behind him, and with me right behind his quilt. We went up the stairs one step at a time, each stair shrieking as we stepped on it.

At the top of the stairs, I dared to breathe once more.

"Cory . . ." I stopped and looked at him more closely. He was panting as though he'd just run home from Jason's. "Are you okay?"

"I guess. Debbie, what're we going to do?"

"Just keep quiet and wait for him to go away."

"What if he comes inside?"

"There isn't much I can do about that," I said. "I can't move Paige, and I don't want to leave her. But we can make sure he doesn't get you. We can hide you up in the attic and tell Dad that you're staying with . . . someone . . . one of your friends at school."

I didn't think much of the idea. It didn't sound like a likely story to me, and it probably wouldn't to Dad. But he'd have to believe it if he couldn't find Cory.

Cory's little hand reached out of the darkness and clutched me by the arm. "Not the attic," he said.

None of us ever went up to the attic in the dark. We didn't much like going up there even in broad daylight.

"We could probably hide you in that big cardboard box so that nobody would be able to find you."

There must have been a better way of putting that. Cory's stubby little fingers dug into me even harder.

"I don't want to stay there forever."

"You won't, silly. There's nothing to stop you from coming out yourself when the coast is clear."

"What about the ghost?"

"You know there isn't any ghost up there."

"No, I don't. We've heard it walking around."

"The house creaks like crazy. All old houses do. That doesn't mean that they have ghosts."

"Well, then how come you don't like to go up there?"

"Because I'm stupid," I said. "Because I'm the biggest fraidy cat in the world. That doesn't mean you have to be, too."

Cory flared up. "I'm not a fraidy cat."

"Prove it!"

I hated myself for attacking a little kid who'd just been through what he'd been through, but I was desperate to make him hide in the attic. Dad might not even think of looking there.

Paige had said once that I acted just like Dad. When I caught myself pressuring Cory into hiding in the attic, I had to admit that maybe she was right. Only it's so hard to explain things to kids, and it's so easy to pull rank on them. Who could blame me?

I stopped short. If it wasn't okay for Dad to do it, then it wasn't okay for me.

"Cory, if Dad finds all of us, he's going to head out on the road fast to make up for lost time. If he finds just Paige and me, he's not so likely to do that. You're the one he wants most. He's going to stick around to look for you. Now just think what it'd be like for Paige to be dragged off to drive all over the country when she's so sick. C'mon Cory, you've got to hide where Dad can't find you."

Cory agreed. We turned and faced the dreaded door to the attic. My hand shook as I turned the knob and inched the door open. It was so dark behind it that I had to feel my way up the stairs and across to where I knew there was a cardboard box about Cory's size.

"If he bumps the box," Cory said in a small voice, "he'll know it's not light like the others."

"You're a smart kid," I said. "But where else can you hide?"

"How about in the newspapers?"

"I don't get what you mean."

"I mean, like we did when we ran away from Dad. Remember, you said he wouldn't look for us where we were because there didn't seem to be any place to hide. Well, I can lie flat in the piles of newspapers Mom put up here for insulation. We can make me a little hole and cover it over with just one or two papers. You get what I mean? It'll be like lying in that little creek bed. . . ."

"You're not only brave," I said, hugging him, "you're also very smart."

We inched our way over under the eaves, felt around and pulled out enough newspapers to make Cory a nest. I hoped there weren't mice who had done the same sort of thing.

"This won't be for long," I said, planting a kiss on the top of his head.

"I guess when you put those papers over me," Cory's little voice came hopefully out of his hole, "even the ghost up here won't know I'm here."

"Actually," I said, "I could do with a friendly ghost about now. I wouldn't mind borrowing one to scare Dad off."

"Feel free to borrow him." Cory's voice was muffled by the newspapers.

I swallowed hard. "Please believe me, Cor. I'd never leave you alone if I thought anything bad would happen to you. Just remember that you're safe when you're invisible, and you're totally invisible now."

I unscrewed the light bulb on my way to the stairs to help guarantee he'd stay invisible.

It's funny how you can control yourself until you start down a flight of stairs, and then suddenly you're sure that all the demons out of hell are just behind you, and you start walking a little faster. Once you start walking faster, you get scareder and scareder till you can't help yourself—you've just got to run.

I didn't exactly run, but for someone in pitch darkness, I was moving pretty fast by the time I got to the bottom of the stairs. In one way, I felt better as soon as I closed the door behind me. But in another, I felt worse. I wouldn't have wanted to be up there alone, and I hated making Cory do what I wouldn't have been willing to do myself.

When I tiptoed back to Paige's bed, I sat down with a sigh of relief and noticed for the first time in my life that darkness could actually be kind of comforting. I felt better just sitting there in the dark, keeping Paige company without actually seeing her, sitting there letting my breath return to normal and listening to her breathe.

Except I wasn't listening to Paige breathing. It was awfully darn quiet in that room. What had happened to her rasping breath and her restless tossing? I strained to hear one sound that would convince me that she was still alive. Not hearing a thing, and dreading what I'd find, I went over to the bed and reached out to touch Paige's still body.

Her skin was cold and wet.

Tears stung my eyes, and I grabbed her as though holding her could bring her back to life.

"Oh, Paige," I whispered hoarsely, "you can't be dead. You don't know how much I'll miss you. What'll I do without you?"

The limp body in my arms made a little sound.

What was going on? I dropped Paige and was reaching for the lamp when Paige's voice froze me in my tracks.

"I'm thirdsty."

"What?"

"I said I'm thirdsty," Paige repeated in a husky voice. "Why'd you have to wake me up, Debbie? Why'd you grab me like thadt?"

I groped around till I found her forehead. It was positively clammy and cold by comparison with how it had felt when she'd been running the fever. I grabbed her again and gave her a big bear hug.

"Hey." She gave me a weak smack on the arm, a mere ghost of the way she used to whomp me when she was well. "Geez, Debbie, wadtch it, will ya?"

"Sorry." I forced myself to let go of her. "I'm so sorry I disturbed you and so glad you're all right."

"I'm not all right," Paige complained. "I told you a million times . . . I'm thirdsty. Can I have some orange juice?"

I'd rather have gotten her water from the upstairs bathroom, but I'd have given her champagne if she'd asked for it.

"Be back in a minute."

"Hey, why dond't you turn on the light?"

"Because Dad's in the neighborhood," I said. "So just keep quiet and keep the lights off. I'll be right back."

At least, I hope I will be, I thought as I picked my way back downstairs and across the living room. I listened for sounds that would tell me if Dad was in the house, but I heard nothing. I slipped quietly into the kitchen and reached up into a cupboard for a mug. Then I reached out quietly for the fridge door.

A blinding flash of light paralyzed me. I stood there, completely stunned, until I finally realized that the light was coming from inside the fridge. That jolted me into action. I jammed my hand inside and over the button that controls the light. Seeing a green haze like northern lights in the sudden darkness after the bright light, I fished around blind for the orange juice, took out the entire pitcher and tried to figure out how I was supposed to close the door without leaking light again for anyone in the yard to see.

I couldn't stay there holding the light button forever, like the Dutch kid who kept his finger in a hole in the dike. Dad was coming quickly, judging from the sweep of his flashlight.

Yes. Dad was standing outside the living room window again. This time, he had a flashlight, and he was probing every corner of the room with its dim light. He was doing it slowly, systematically, raking the room in straight lines that steadily came closer and closer to the kitchen.

I broke out in a cold sweat as I tried to reach around behind the fridge for the electrical cord so I could pull the plug. I strained and my fingertips brushed something I thought was it, but it was no use.

I bit my lip. In that dark house, a flash of light from the kitchen would be as noticeable as lightning against the night sky.

I reached into the kitchen drawer next to the fridge. No, no scotch tape there after all. But there had to be! That was where Mom kept it, and she hadn't emptied the drawer yet.

I felt around some more, and my knuckle brushed the rough edge of the thing that cuts the tape. Yes, we had tape. Now if I could just pull it out and tear it off, one-handed. If it would just stick well enough to hold down the stupid button.

It did.

I eased the door shut, grabbed the pitcher of orange juice and the mug to put it in, and rolled across the kitchen floor to a shadowy spot between the kitchen and the living room.

Less than a second later, a light from the window over the sink raked the fridge where I'd been and went carefully over the kitchen, inch by inch.

Eventually, the light moved on—I could hear Dad checking out the back porch—and I crawled to the stairs with the orange juice for Paige. She was sound asleep by the time I got back to her.

Something in me broke down in that kitchen. I don't know what it was. All I know is that I was suddenly furious that anybody or anything had been able to make me that afraid. I was angry enough to attack Dad. Or at least to fight him if he did get inside and come for us.

I put down the orange juice beside the bed and went back up to the attic for Cory.

"Psst. Cory, you can come out now if you want to."

"Has Dad gone?"

"No, not yet. But I've had a better idea. I'm going to put us all in the same room and block off the door. If I have to, I'll use your baseball bat to keep Dad away."

"You're crazy!"

"You think so? Good. If I look crazy enough, Dad'll be more likely not to tangle with me."

"Do you know what a mess a baseball bat would make if you ever hit anybody?" Cory asked.

"If I look ready to swing the bat, I probably won't have to. But don't worry. . . . I don't want to kill anybody. I'd break his leg, maybe, but—"

"Even that would surprise Dad," Cory said.

We looked at each other and sputtered into laughter.

We made ourselves a kind of fortress in the room where Paige lay sleeping. Soon, Cory lay sleeping there, too, while I kept watch alone.

It was then that maybe I should have felt worse than I'd ever felt in my life before. After all, I was determined to fight my father if I had to. But I didn't feel worse. I actually felt better. Maybe even pretty good.

That was when I understood what it was that frail little Mr. Andover had made me feel. He had made me feel that weak people could win. That maybe life wasn't so scary after all.

I was tired of being afraid. Being afraid didn't keep me safe; it just wore me out and tore me down. And maybe my being afraid made it easier for people to do bad things to me.

When I stood up to Dad . . .

I shivered. How could I stand up to him?

I straightened my shoulders and clenched my fists. I could. I already had.

And I had won, too. I knew it when I heard the clanking of Dad's old car fading in the distance as he drove away.

MOM GOT HOME around noon the next day and listened to our story and hugged us tight. Then she called her lawyer.

"Listen, Roz, I got home to find the kids here . . . alone. I want a restraining order against Tyler A.S.A.P."

Paige was calling down for some ginger ale, and Mom was just signaling me to take her some when she glanced over my shoulder and said, "I'll get back to you. He's here. He's standing at the front door right now."

I turned and there he was, looking half dead and about a hundred years old.

"Go see to Paige," Mom said, shooing me away nervously. For my part, I was glad to have something to do somewhere else at that moment.

But when I could hear voices raised downstairs five minutes later, I began to feel all tight and restless. After all we'd been through, I couldn't believe that I was up there trying to catch snatches of what they were saying, just like I'd always done.

"I should go down there and help Mom," I said to Paige.

"Shh. I'm trying to lidsen."

Dad was saying, "I took good care of them. My God, you'd think I'd mistreated them!"

Mom was crying, and her voice sounded strangled. "I hate you. You're irresponsible, a big bully and—"

Suddenly I was sure that I could help.

"Where are you going? Debbie! Come back here!" said Paige.

But I was on my way downstairs to the living room.

Both Mom and Dad looked at me as though they thought I'd lost my mind. Who can blame them? I thought I'd lost it, too.

"Mom. Dad. I've got to talk to you."

"Not now, Debbie," Mom said. "We're talking. Go see where Cory is and—"

"There's something I've got to say."

"Listen to your mother, Deb," Dad said. "This doesn't concern you."

"You know that isn't true." Now they were listening. "How can you say that when it's us you're fighting about? Please listen to me. Before I lose my nerve."

"As though you would ever lose your nerve."

He said it with a lopsided smile, and I was stunned at the thought that my father actually seemed to think I had a lot of nerve. And the right kind of nerve at that.

"I'm the world's biggest coward," I said.

Suddenly, his eyes looked kind of red around the rims. "Yeah, I noticed that—the way you fought me every step of the way. I gave it my best shot, but you won. And now I'm just too bloody tired to fight you anymore."

"Dad . . . I am . . . I have been . . . really, really scared. You scared me. You scared us—all of us—and . . ." Don't tell me I was going to cry! I never cry! But tears were already spilling over. "And, Dad . . . I hate being scared of you . . . of my own father."

"Oh, Deb," he said in an odd, husky voice. "Why do you suppose mothers say 'Wait till your father gets home'? It's our job to be scary . . . to keep our kids in line."

Mom turned on him then. "That's a really dumb thing to say, Ty. That kind of father went out of fashion fifty years ago."

"I guess I'm an old-fashioned kind of father."

That's when I yelled, "No. You come across more like a giant, scary baby than a father!"

Dad's neck corded up and his face darkened. I tightened up, waiting for him to come across the room at me, but he didn't. Instead, he seemed to deflate. He stood there biting his lip.

"You say you love us, but you don't care about anything but making us do what you want us to do—no matter how cruel you have to be."

"I would never hurt you, you know."

"But you did! I know you didn't hit me, but when you twisted everything around so that I looked like an idiot—or a liar—in front of the policeman—"

Dad interrupted with, "I know I haven't always been the world's greatest dad, but there are a lot worse. I did my best."

"I want a chance to be a kid. How can we be kids if you won't stop being one?"

"You're saying I act like a kid? If you could have seen how I searched for you—nearly going out of my mind—up and down the whole network of trails, searching for you from dawn to dusk for two days just in case maybe, just maybe, you hadn't lit out for home. In case maybe you really were lost."

"Is that all you care about? How you felt?" I could barely hear my own voice, but Dad was watching my face and something in it stopped him short as surely as if I had screamed.

"You're a fool, Tyler." Mom's voice was quiet but deathly angry. "They wouldn't have been out on those trails if you hadn't kidnapped them. Kidnapped them. An indictable offense."

For a minute, I thought he was going to blow. Maybe hit Mom. But then he deflated still more.

"If you had any idea what went through my mind when I thought maybe you were dead and it was all my fault . . ."

"It was your fault," Mom said.

But Dad didn't explode at this either. Instead, his voice became just a whisper. "I know."

He turned to me. "At first . . . well, it's just a good thing I didn't find you at first, Deb, because I was too furious to think straight. But after a while, all that mattered was that you guys were safe. I thought I'd find you in Yellowstone or at the border. When I didn't, I really didn't think I'd ever see you again. That was the worst moment of my life."

He scrubbed his face with his hand. "The last five days have been one continuous nightmare."

I looked into his brown eyes so exactly like my own, and I suddenly blurted out, "I'm sorry you were worried."

"Yes. Well you should be!"

Mom bristled. "When will you ever get it through your thick skull that you're the one to blame here?"

Dad dredged up a weak grin. "Oh, Ann, give me a break. I've just said I realized that, haven't I?"

He turned to me. "I thought I knew what was best for you. It wasn't what you wanted. I should have listened. It would have been smart to have listened. From here on in, I'll listen."

"I'll believe it when it happens," I said, but I felt some of the anger seep out of me.

Dad held out his arms. "I'll forgive you if you'll forgive me."

I didn't run to his arms. I'm not Paige and I never will be. I took a step backward. "It's going to take awhile."

He dropped his arms. "I know. Hey, listen. We'll work it out."

I almost started telling him what he'd have to do if he ever hoped to get close to any of us again, but I stopped myself. I'd been in charge long enough . . . too long. I had Mom. Mom had her lawyer. This wasn't something it was up to me to fix. For once in my life, I was going to leave the room and not even listen outside the door.

Could I do it? Could I let the grownups be grownups without my help? It was risky. Then I looked again at Dad and how beaten he seemed. He sure hadn't looked like that before we went missing.

Maybe Dad was growing up.

I guess we all grew up a lot that horrible summer.

I wish I knew Mr. Andover's address so I could let him know that at least one father and his kids did manage to keep talking to each other in spite of everything. It hasn't been easy, but we're still working on it. And that's something.

ABOUT THE AUTHOR

CHERYLYN STACEY began writing stories in 1989. Her first novel for young adults, *I'll Tell You Tuesday If I Last that Long,* received a Canadian Children's Book Centre Our Choice Award. Cherylyn Stacey also has written an award-winning screenplay, and taught high school, college and university. When she's not writing, reading or teaching, she travels with her two daughters. She lives and works in Edmonton, Alberta.